flying leap

flying leap

a novel in perspective

RALF W. OLIVER

Two Harbors Press

Two Harbors Press
212 3rd Avenue North, Suite 290
Minneapolis, MN 55401
612.455.2293
www.TwoHarborsPress.com

ISBN-13: 978-1-937928-00-1
LCCN: 2011944439

Distributed by Itasca Books

Cover Photo by Jennifer Sabet
Cover Design by Madge Duffy
Typeset by Tim Parlin

Printed in the United States of America

To the love of my life, Kate. This would not exist without you. To my parents who chose to have me. And to all the people throughout my life that have been a part in this experience.

Thank you.

mp

He glanced down; it seemed a lot higher up than from below. Funny, how things changed with a simple shift of perspective. Perspective. That was something to consider ... it was a bit too late now though, he had made up his mind and that was that. He had been a decision-maker all his life.

* * *

"So what do these guys want exactly?" he asked.

Everyone in the boardroom shifted nervously. No one really knew exactly, but they weren't about to tell their boss that. He could tell what was going on. He liked it too. He loved the fact that he could feel his way around the room. They liked him. But they also were nervous in just that right amount.

"Anyone have an idea?" he asked with mock inquisitiveness. He was curious to find out who would step up. Bryan, his COO, cleared his throat. He had brought Bryan into his new venture two years ago because he trusted him, and because Bryan was very smart and knew how to run a business. Having Bryan on board helped him achieve all his ideas regarding the business and made him look better as well.

"Well," Bryan said, "they are looking for us to buy them up is what it boils down to. I think they're good guys and have a brilliant idea … they've tried the VC route and haven't had any serious nibbles and they like us—well, *you* and what you've done—and they think that you get what they are up to and would be interested."

He turned in his chair and looked out the window.

"And no one but Bryan felt comfortable enough to tell me this?" He shook his head, turned and smiled at everyone in the room. "What do I pay you for anyways? Come on guys, did you think I was going to fire you or what?" The feeling in the room was uneasy now—just how it should be. The next thing he would say was very important; his team was waiting. He showed his teeth and laughed. "Am I some egomaniacal power monger who wants a bunch of scared yea-sayers? I don't think so. As a matter of fact, if you don't step up and tell me what you really think, I *will* fire you!"

They all laughed, some with a real sense of levity, some with uneasiness. Good, that's what he wanted. Always keep them guessing.

"Well, Bryan, thanks for the info, I'll think about it. Leave me the proposal and I'll deal with it yet tonight. Meeting adjourned, everybody go home. Don't you have lives to live?"

* * *

He could have just picked up the phone later that evening and had Bryan take care of it, for the benefit or to the detriment of the guys and their proposal. Their lives would be affected no matter what his decision.

This was a powerful feeling, something he had gotten used to surprisingly quickly, something he could not have anticipated, especially this early in his life. He was in his mid-thirties and considered himself "healthily wealthy." When he sold his first company he had only been twenty-three chronologically but maybe seventeen psychologically.

None of this was of any use to anyone now, least of all himself.

Looking out the window of his office in midtown Manhattan, he had one of his restless moments of reflection, when he wasn't sure of anything at all. He couldn't even quite put his finger on it, but unsure he was, and of what exactly had been a question that was running through his mind like the echo of something he almost had known at one point. Whenever he began

3

to think along those lines his mind began the battle between contemplation and rationale; on the one hand the feeling of uncertainty, slightly uncomfortable at best and downright disturbing at worst, and on the other the rational process of dismantling this incomplete feeling into its smallest of parts only to discard it in a whirlwind of reassuring but all too familiar thoughts of reason.

Thus ridding his mind quickly and efficiently of his momentary lapse of reason he returned to his train of thought once again and decided to not make the call after all. This could wait until tomorrow, they could wait until tomorrow, completely foregoing his commitment from years earlier when he had struggled to secure funding for his first business endeavor and would sit around for seeming eternities waiting for money people to call him back, waiting for any one person of importance to call him back, and swearing to God personally that he would never make anyone in this position wait for an answer as he had had to. Just another echo in his mind from long ago at this moment; right now sushi at his favorite place with his friends sounded more important and most certainly more certain than the uncertainty he was experiencing right now.

He picked up his trusty iPhone, gathered his keys and briefcase, and called downstairs to the garage

4

for his car to be brought up. Once he left his office the eerie silence that surrounded him in the larger space of the floor with all its empty cubicles made him uneasy for a second; a frequent recognition that his life was maybe not as full as he liked himself to believe. But as usual, a little body shake rid himself of the uneasiness and he went straight towards the elevators.

He got down to the garage and waited for Raul to bring the car around. Raul was the valet who took care of his car—in fact, the only one allowed to do so. His car was a beauty and joy. It wasn't the usual rich boy's toy of show-offingness that most of his friends drove; it was a VW, a Phaeton, which had cost him sixty-five grand. It had that little extra cache, the touch that an obvious choice of other German carmakers just didn't have. Plus, it gave the impression that he really didn't care about what other people thought, and that was really important to him. The inherent oxymoronic nature of this actually eluded him.

Raul drove up and held the door open for him. He didn't get in.

"How is your wife doing, Raul, how's Julius?"

Raul's wife had had some major complications during her pregnancy with their child and he had found out about it through one of Raul's colleagues. When he heard that Raul had no health insurance, he put him on his company's payroll. He had also felt compelled to pay their medical bills until the insurance kicked in. It was the decent thing to do, to be nice to people whose station in life was less fortunate than your own. It had been one of his core beliefs; he hated arrogant people who were holier than thou. Raul's wife had to be on bed rest for the last two months of pregnancy but eventually delivered a healthy son.

Raul beamed at him. "He is doing so much better! I cannot thank you enough for everything you have done for me and my family. I don't know how to repay you. You have been so kind and generous. I wish more people were like you."

He shook Raul's hand. "Raul, please, anyone in my position would have done the same. I am just glad that your wife and son are okay." He got in the car.

"Make sure to email me some pictures of little Julius, will ya?" He winked at Raul and smiled. "Do you need anything, my friend? Some meds? Toys? Diapers? A vacation?"

Raul laughed and put up his hands. "No sir, please, you have done so much. We are fine." He knew that wasn't true, that Raul's family was struggling to make ends meet. He waived and drove out of the garage.

As he was driving to the sushi restaurant, he called his assistant, Bridget. "Hey Bridge, sorry to bother you so late, but I want you to have a bonus check issued for employee number 00 in the amount of $2500 tomorrow and make sure he gets it right away."

"No problem, Boss, your wish is my command. I will make sure it gets handled correctly through HR."

"Beautiful."

"You know, I think it's pretty awesome what you're doing for Raul. I think we should put it in the newsletter."

"No way! You hear me Bridge? Absolutely not. I count on your magical powers to keep this a secret. You're the best. Now get back to whatever it is you were doing. I'll see you tomorrow."

As he hung up he smiled; he knew that Bridget had been talking to people behind his back about his good deed, and that made his act of kindness that much more meaningful and potent. This way people saw him as a good guy at heart, which gave him more room to be a ball buster when he had to be.

He spent that evening talking and eating with his friends, checking out the scene in the restaurant, humbly feeling full of himself as he thought the spiritually evolved person would. His banter was intelligent, funny, and witty, and he had perfected the art of asking people questions about anything at all that he wanted to influence and control, including people.

Innocent questions.

He asked his girlfriend these questions a lot.

"Did I tell you already that Josh had some extra shoes he got from the show?" he'd ask her. Josh was a "friend" of his, meaning they both were benefiting in some way from knowing each other. Josh was an up-and-coming fashion designer who was quickly turning into a hot ticket around town and his shoes were in great demand. He kept a few "high potentials" around in his life at any given time; some of them could turn into someone and then it was very valuable to have known them before they were somebody—people trusted you that way. If after a couple of years nothing came of them, he would stop returning their calls and let them slowly fade out of his life, no harm done.

He knew full well that he had not only asked her the question a few times in the past couple of days, but he had gotten very good at pretending to be so "in the moment" that he would forget things like that all the time. He almost believed it himself at this point, which made it that much easier to fool people; so the question got asked until the person would respond in the way he had wanted them to in the first place.

8

"Yes, you have a couple of times, honey," his girl-friend would say. "Would you like me to go check them out?"

"No, no, it's not about that, Sweetie, I just couldn't remember whether I told you already. Only go if you want to."

"Well, maybe I will." Soon she would realize what a great opportunity this was to score free hot-ticket shoes and this way it was her idea now. And she would look good thanks to him and tell people about his friendship with Josh.

This was his M.O., he did this in his business as well, always ahead of everyone else, having to some-times guide in a direct way, but most of the time influ-encing others with this subtle questioning, ensuring that people would eventually believe he had nothing to do with it, but of course they would see his ques-tions as their inspiration to act and would end up at least thanking him or at best giving him credit for their insight. And if things went into the shitter, he could always claim that it had been their idea after all, he hadn't told them what to do. It was brilliant.

He had been blessed with a great sense of intu-ition; it was second nature for him to meet someone, extend his energetic tentacles, and read them. Not really of course. But get a very good sense about them and their strengths and weaknesses. It was automatic. He could tune in well and know exactly how to approach them to his advantage. Size them up. It was not often that he ran into people who could hold their own in that realm; most of humanity was way too asleep in his mind to even notice what he was doing with them, and most of the time he was right. When he didn't like someone, he would collect useful information for later use: the kind that was discrediting, belittling, or disheartening in general. But he always did it in such a way that they couldn't connect anything back to him. He could always claim innocence.

This was not crude backstabbing or badmouthing, mind you. This was an art, one crafted with subtle but powerful energies that showed up in all kinds of ways. So much more effective than anything obviously directed at someone. And much easier as a device to make people realize whatever you needed them to realize "on their own."

Thus had been the life he had led. He had become successful and had made those in his favor succeed as well, but all at a spiritual cost he failed to understand. He thought of himself as incredibly spiritual and humble and reflective and all that. He had read all the books about presence and silence and contemplation, he could talk a spiritual game so well that even some of his closest friends bought it hook, line, and sinker. A fact that in the larger scheme of things did not serve him well, because he eventually believed it himself.

* * *

He looked down over the edge of the building again. He was preparing himself to jump.

The past few weeks had not been good; his company had gone belly up after his very creative accountant had created his way into the Cayman Islands, or somewhere else warm and sunny he was sure, with all his money. He had tried to turn things around, to change it, to influence it into what it needed to be, but to no avail. Thanks to his money troubles, his girlfriend had left him. He was still able to almost convince her that it was her issues that made her leave, but he had had moments of doubt even then.

Once the financial troubles began he tried with all his might and spiritual understanding to "uncreate" the mess he felt he had nothing to do with. He had trusted that asshole with all the finances, his personal and the company's. And this is what he got in return? Betrayal?! Unbelievable.

He was an enlightened being amongst the asleep and he couldn't stand the loneliness anymore. Moving on to the next stage was the smartest thing to do. He was not afraid to die. He did not claim to know what was coming, but he was clear on the fact that it was not some all or nothing, brimstone and fire or glory and heaven deal.

Again, the oxymoronic nature of this eluded him.

So here he stood, ready to go. Just a few more minutes maybe. Being up here was really peaceful. New York was having one of those early spring days with that hint of the approaching summer in the air, when everything looked sort of cleaner, the sky was a deep blue and everyone in the city was feeling a little more friendly and beautiful, even more connected maybe. A breeze went around his face and for the first time in months he noticed that too and enjoyed it.

Maybe he could create that feeling after he left this plane of existence. That would be nice, living in this feeling of a perfect kind of day. He was sure that all of life was ultimately just a feeling, never actually physical, so "dying" just meant moving into that feeling completely and living there forever.

"Well, *being* in that feeling would serve you better. The living thing you got going there would almost certainly keep you attached," said a voice.

He looked around. There was no one there. "Hello? Someone there?" The rooftop was empty. Forget it. Probably just nerves; he was about to end his life after all. He straightened up and stepped closer to the edge and looked over it again. He had never been afraid of heights, he had even done some skydiving, just enough to be able to say that he had really done it, about twenty jumps, but that was enough to be able to talk about it and interest people. To bore people was by far the biggest waste of energy he figured. But looking over the edge now he had a queasy feeling in his stomach ... never had had it on the plane before he would jump out ... weird.

He took in a deep breath and noticed it. Breathing. Man, humans did it all of their lives and never even noticed it, unless they were being robbed of the opportunity. He took a step up on the elevated edge of the building. He stretched out his arms, and let himself feel, really feel, everything around him.

And then he began to cry. Really cry. He got down on all fours and began to wail, in a way he never had before in his life, and at that moment it became a one hundred percent certainty, if there had been any doubt before, now he knew with every fiber of his being: he had to die.

* * *

"Oh yes, you do, just maybe not the way you think you need to." The voice again.

"What the hell is going on here?" He forgot he was crying. "Don't fuck with me like that! Who is this?"

"I'm right here, you idiot! Just open your eyes."

13

flying leap

What the hell was going on? Was he going mental or something? Well, he was about to commit suicide, that qualified. Maybe this was what happened to people who were about to kill themselves. The mind shut down in preparation.

"That's actually one way to look at it, never have quite thought of it that way," said the voice. He couldn't tell where it was coming from.

"Of course you can't tell where it's coming from, you've been blind all your life. I am not surprised you're deaf as well."

"Okay, I am officially crazy. Who is this?" He did his body shake and refocused, wiping the snot and tears from his face. Then he considered the only plausible answer in his mind.

"Is this ... God?"

A snicker. He got a snicker in response. Great.

"Not quite. At least not in the way that you are considering it right now. I'm right here, just open your eyes!"

He opened his eyes really wide and looked around with intense focus. He must have looked like a complete moron.

"Not literally open your eyes, you idiot! Just see me." There was nothing here but a rooftop, gravel, steel, AC units, wires and antennas, a pigeon, and him.

"Aha," said the voice, "getting warmer. You really are a little dense, aren't you?"

His eyes locked in on the pigeon. Its eyes weren't just black and indistinguishable as he had always seen them; there was something else there.

"It's called consciousness—what you're seeing," said the voice.

"Are you kidding me?! A talking pigeon, yeah right, this is what it must be like when people are on some kind of trip ... " He had never done a drug in his life, so he really didn't know.

"That has been one of the truly authentic things about you, not doing drugs."

"Alright, enough with this already. A pigeon can't talk, or if it could it most certainly wouldn't be able to hold a conversation!" What was he saying?

"What *are* you saying?" asked the voice. "You are correct in that I am not actually talking to you in the classic sense. I am not using the physical properties of sound anyways—you would have trouble understanding pigeon lingo, comes with the territory so to speak, though sometimes allowances can be made, if it's really important. What I am getting at here is that I am *communicating* with you, though not *talking* to you."

He stood there completely dumbfounded and didn't know what to do. Maybe he should just take a flying leap off the building.

"Too much thinking is what got you in this mess in the first place, my friend. Go ahead and jump, it's your choice entirely, I have no issue with this, but I also wanted to offer you an ear, though technically pigeons don't have ears."

"Are you reading my mind?" he asked incredulously.

"Not exactly, but as I mentioned a moment ago, we are communicating, so a certain frequency of consciousness is being utilized here. Thus I am not reading your mind, we're just tuned in to a particular frequency."

"How could a pigeon know that?" He couldn't believe he was having this conversation.

"I can appreciate your disbelief, but your choices at this moment in your life have enabled you to connect with me, although 'me' is a very loose concept here. I'm not really a pigeon, though I am that as well."

This was getting a little too strange. Maybe he should just get back to the business of dying.

"As I have said, that's fine, in fact you are dead-on accurate with your whole 'having to die' thing." It snickered again. "Pardon the pun. Only, there are many different *ways* to die, and I can see that you have contemplated another way to die here, though you haven't quite caught on yet." And then it added with an invisible but definite smile: "As I said, you're a little bit dense."

"Excuse me? If I was so dense, how could I have been so successful in my life and achieve all that I have achieved? Someone dense doesn't achieve like that!"

"And this from a guy who has, by his own standards, nothing to show for his achievements and thus is ready to jump off a building, because he knows he has to die, but won't even take a moment to consider the many facets of that statement? What do you think 'dying' is? I would reckon that this is as good a time as any to reflect on this."

It had a point. What did he have to show for his life? Why was he up here? Had he not always known that all his stuff didn't mean anything and he could do without it all if push came to shove? Now that it was gone, he was about to jump. That *was* dense, or at least he didn't show any follow through, which was something he always had done. It was something he expected out of his people as well. Without follow through you couldn't achieve anything. So why wasn't he following through on his own life here? He had lost it all, but so what?

"My God, you ramble a lot, it's very draining to watch and experience. Do you even notice this incessant thinking you do?" interrupted the pigeon. "But I digress, Mr. Dense. So, *have* you considered that there are many ways to die?"

"Not really, no, I guess I just figured that jumping was pretty painless. I've read before that they believe that our mind shuts down before we ever hit the ground, and I figured it was a pretty safe bet. I mean with sleeping pills someone could find you or you don't take enough and just wake up five days later with a big fucking headache; guns are messy and you could turn yourself into a vegetable if you miss by this much"—he held up two fingers—"and I didn't want to risk others getting hurt. Drowning I wouldn't be able to pull off I think … "

"Okay, your Royal Highness of Denseville, I meant that there are many different forms of dying."

"I know what you meant, Mister … " he struggled to think of something witty. "Birdbrain."

"Let me assure you, you do not."

* * *

His life thus far certainly hadn't been hard by any means, he had grown up in a middle-class household with reasonably happy parents, normal dysfunction (his dad had been an alcoholic until he was about ten), an older sister he was pretty close to, and the average disdain for family gatherings and holidays.

All would have added up to a pretty average life if it hadn't been for his mother and grandmother telling him constantly in many different ways that he always needed to listen to his "inner voice." This was a sort of mantra that continued throughout his childhood and became something of a given in his mind: that there was such a thing as an inner voice and that it was a good idea to listen to it, lest it tell you that you are Jesus or that you should kill all red-haired women or something of that nature.

He had been very close to his maternal grandmother; she lived about three hours away from home, so he didn't get to see her as often as he would have liked. The woman knew how to laugh and used to tell him (apart from the inner voice thing) to never forget that "life was terminal," and why would you get serious about something if you would not even get out alive in the end. She had made sense to him.

Education was valued in his family and so he figured out early how to get by with just doing enough so he could hold his own around just about anyone whilst also being able to sound smart about something when in fact he had no clue. In addition he had been very lucky. The perfect setup for a life of illusion.

Things went well by all exterior measures. His inner voice occasionally gave him some nice tips that

he managed to catch in between his incessant thinking, so that he had made enough decisions to end up
in the right place at the right time. When he was in
grad school and the early craze of the Internet boom
was in full swing, he had created an "idea website," a
clearinghouse of sorts for people who had new ideas
to meet up with others who were interested in buying into those ideas and marketing them. Within a
year he took the business public and sold it for $58
million a few months later. The site went dead within six months—lucky again. He then proceeded to
piss some of the money away, invested in some not-
so-smart ideas, and ended up with his last company
that was supposed to revolutionize communication
via the Internet. Of course, before things could really
come to fruition, his accountant had gotten creative.

During all these years he had pretended his life
and everything in it. He was masterful at making
people feel at ease and appreciated, and sometimes
he could be authentic and even genuinely like someone. But most of his life was spent faking it in some
way or another, always running a self-serving purpose in the background. He even managed to do this
with his girlfriends and his friends, except the ones
he had known all his life, but even then he faked it
enough, never fully there in a way. The worst part in
all of this was that he had been doing it to himself as

well and had no clue, none whatsoever, that this was going on. Tricky business.

This was the first time in his life he became fully aware of all this. He wasn't sure what to do with this information, when he remembered that he was sitting on a rooftop in Manhattan, ready to jump, while taking a break talking to a flying rat, and an insulting one at that.

"Insulting?!" said the bird. "And I am a *pigeon*, thank you very much."

"You are still here then? And this is happening?"

"Well, yes, and very interesting insights you've been having there, by the way. Quite a bit to chew, isn't it?" It tilted its head on that last remark, sort of like the "Am I right or am I right?" tilt usually reserved for humans. This was weird.

"Welcome to weirdness then, pull up a chair and relax ... " He looked around with one eyebrow raised. "Figuratively speaking," the bird added. This time he had to laugh.

"You're one smart dove, if I may say so." He was still a little uneasy talking to a bird.

"I'll take the *dove*, thank you very much; and why are you so uneasy? You were about to jump off a building, I think you are beyond *uneasy*, my friend. Welcome to the world of where the impossible is possible, the real becomes the illusion, and you discover there is something else going on."

He perked up. "What did you just say?"

"Which part exactly?" Mr. Dove inquired.

"The part about something else going on. I have had the feeling that somehow there *is* something else going on all my life. As if I could feel another dimension or reality that was going on right under my nose, but I could never quite touch it or see it. I don't know how to explain it."

"You're doing a great job in my book. And you know what, my dimwitted friend, I am here to tell you that there is something going on, and if you're interested, we'll explore it together." It scratched its two feet in the gravel with grave importance—at least that's what it looked like to him.

"This is nuts, man! How do I know that I am not having a psychotic break or something. I mean, I'm sorry, I am talking—correction—*communicating* with a flying—sorry—pigeon, and you're in my head for crying out loud!" He would have laughed had it not been so absolutely real and surreal at the same time.

"What does it matter what you call this? As long as we're having a good time, the conversation is flowing, and you're learning something new in the process, where's the harm in that?" The bird made sense, but it was still a bird, for Pete's sake. "And you're not having a psychotic break. As long as you can still ask yourself that, you're fine." It snickered again. "Though I would say you qualify for unstable, I mean, look at yourself—you were ready to jump a couple of minutes ago."

"Maybe I still am," he mumbled.

"Oh, come on now, pull up the proverbial chair and let's have some fun. You can still jump at any time, the ledge is right over there. What have you got to lose, my friend?"

Nothing. Absolutely nothing. There was nothing left to lose, the bird was right, but this was also the depressing part—he had nothing left. Nothing to lose and everything to gain, he had heard that many times before. Made sense now. What to do, what to do? By every measure of an intelligent and lucid mind, this was crazy or at the very least impossible. Birds didn't talk or communicate or snicker or tilt their heads meaningfully, but it was happening, or at least it was happening in his mind.

"If I may interrupt for a second, incessant rambler boy, that's a very good place to start!"

"Start what exactly?" he asked. What was it talking about? He was in the throes of ending, not starting something, unless you considered what followed physical death to be a new beginning.

"A conversation. About what is going on and this

23

feeling you have had all your life." The bird tilted its head again. He was beginning to get used to this.

What could you possibly tell me about that? he wondered. "I am not even sure what the hell I am talking about when I talk about this ... this feeling. Who knows whether something like that is even real."

"Let's revisit that whole death business first. Do you remember?"

"Something about me deciding *how* to kill myself ... "

The bird looked at him with that mental nudge expression that said "And ... ?"

"I don't remember! My brain does ramble a lot I guess. I was telling you about all the different ways I could go about the killing business and you said that there were many different ways to kill oneself, and I said that I got it—and you insisted on me being dense, thank you very much."

"That is correct. You weren't getting it." The bird gave an important pause. "Let me ask you something: do you think that the only way that death can be experienced is by killing your body?" Non-existent raised eyebrows again.

He took a deep and exasperated breath. "Dying implies the ending of my physical and psychological existence."

"You are sure about that?"

"Yeah, I'm sure, and if you don't get to your point I will show you in a second what I mean, okay?" He was eyeing the ledge with an "I dare you" look on his face.

The pigeon managed to look as if it were rolling its black eyes. "The *point* is that there may be more ways of dying than you have considered."

"All I know is that if I had jumped already, I wouldn't be *here* anymore, because Kansas would go bye bye." He felt this was bringing him back to some sense of reality, that telling himself this was making the situation more reasonable, more normal. At least the pigeon existed, though he couldn't figure out where the communication really belonged.

"New York would go bye bye, but that's exactly what I would like to examine. Why do you think you started to cry so violently earlier?"

"I don't know, I've never done anything like this before; I have no clue whether this is a normal part of the suicide process." This was the most surreal thing he had ever experienced. At this moment, he was sure that he couldn't be sure of anything anymore, nothing seemed to stick to his mind, and grabbing onto a thought was like trying to grab slippery squid with chopsticks, which he had tried (successfully, of course) in China on a business trip. The point was it was almost impossible. Now he was unable to hold on to his thinking, it was a mess. It felt as though he was slipping through his mental hands, as if the person he had been was disappearing—no, dissolving— in front of his eyes.

"That's what I'm talking about!" said the bird, and he knew that if it was physically possible, it would have crossed its wings in front of its body and leaned back against the wall, very happy with itself.

* * *

What the hell was it talking about? That he was already dead even before he actually jumped off the roof? That he was not connected to his body somehow?

Out of the blue he saw himself standing in front of the open casket at his grandfather's funeral (the paternal one, whom he was very close to as well, he wasn't funny like his maternal grandmother, but he taught him a lot about the rules of life and had been sort of a dad to him when his actual dad was busy being drunk most of the time), and realized with utter clarity in his ten-year-old mind that his grandfather was no longer there, not only not in that body, but literally had never been that body. He had *inhabited* that body, but he had never been that body. Was that what the bird was getting at?

26

"Yes!" cried the pigeon with slight indignation.

"Okay, I'm with you, we aren't our bodies, but we inhabit them. I can go with that." He considered the ramifications. "But then what am I, and even more importantly, where am I?"

"That depends on when."

"When? Where I am depends on when I am? What? You are way out there now, my man, you're losing me fast on this trip into lala land." He had to laugh—this would have been really funny if he lived in Los Angeles instead of New York.

"It would have been," agreed the bird. "Let me explain what I mean. The when is referring to a point in time, given that you are looking at things through a time lens. From that vantage point, the question of where you are is intimately connected to when you are in time. Before birth, where are you? During your lifetime, where are you at any particular time? Are you always where your body is at any given point in time? Have you not found yourself wandering off in your mind, only to find yourself back in your body again? Where are you when you sleep? Or better yet, when you dream? And after you leave the body, where and when are you? Do you only exist within time? As you just said yourself, we inhabit our bodies, which means that there is something or someone making this statement. And that goes with your experience of your grandfather's body: his body was there, but *he* was not, thus he existed *beyond* the body, didn't he? What and when is this being that is conscious and aware of the life you experience? Everyone else on earth is in the same boat."

Whoa. He thought that he was intelligent enough, but this bird was doing a great job messing with his mind. But he was game. He had nowhere else to go. So he decided to stick around to give this wild ride or whatever he was on here on this rooftop in the middle of Manhattan a serious try. He could always jump later.

"That sorta went over my head, to tell you the truth. What I can gather is that I am not my body, but inhabit it, and that time is a very loose concept when it comes to me and my body. Is that right?"

"Yes, that's about right." The bird simply looked at him. This was not going to be easy.

"So, what does it *mean*?" His head was swimming, and hurt like it did after a really bad flu.

"What do you think it means?"

"Oh no, I am not in therapy here, not with a fuckin' bird, no offense, but don't start me with that 'how does that make you feel' and 'what do you think' bullshit. If I knew how I felt or what I thought, I wouldn't have asked!"

"None taken." That was it. Nothing else. It just

sat there and looked as though it were bored.

"What?!" he demanded.

"What what?"

"Oh for God's sake, I'll just get busy jumping then, don't think I'm not ready to go." No reaction. This wasn't going anywhere. He was probably insane after all, talking to a bird. But why was this happening at all? How was it happening? The bird was right there in front of him, but its voice was in his mind, he wasn't hearing it, or was he? It just wasn't making any sense. He noticed his head hurting again and sat back against the ledge and took a deep breath. Breathing. There it was again.

Suddenly he had a thought. Who was aware of his breathing right now? "Me," was the obvious answer, but at the same time he was aware of his thinking about the breathing, about the pain in his head, his messed-up mind, his desperation, his wish to end it all, but how could he be *aware* of all those things and do them at the same time? Who was being aware of the Me? He had never asked himself that before. Was he experiencing a multiple personality disorder? No, it all still felt pretty much like him in there. What on earth was going on?

"Now that you're willing to entertain something a bit outside of your usual experience, and have indeed come up with one version of how it does or doesn't make sense to you, let's explore." The bird popped back in his mind, and landed on his right knee, looking right at him. Scared the crap out of him; he hadn't even noticed it fly.

"And why do you think that may have been, my friend? Because you were so lost in your mind that you did not notice your body. Just as though you were gone from your body at that moment. This is all I meant to say earlier, just as an example, a starting point, a mere beginning of something for you to play with further."

"Just don't scare me like that again, alright?" His heart was still beating out of sync.

"Then I suggest you stay present." It was pointing its head forward like a human would prod you with their finger to gently but clearly make a point.

Present. Stay present. He had always thought of himself as a present person—whenever he was with other people he was very aware of what they were doing and saying, always was engaged in the conversation, a good listener and all that. Something else snuck into his mind right then: what if he had actually never *been* present, but had only *acted* present? After all, when around other people, he had always been thinking about his own agenda in some way, about what to say next, to somehow sound as though he had listened or to show how much he knew about the subject at hand. Or he had been thinking about how he could get away from the conversation, how he could one-up the person, how he could get them to like him, how that might help him in the future. Oh my God, he had never been present, it had always been about him, even when he thought that it was about the other person. Holy crap.

"Mmm," said the bird in agreement.

It was as though a floodgate had opened in his mind, and the rooftop, the bird, the current moment, they all disappeared and he saw himself throughout his life manipulating everything and everyone, and then it hit him like a ton of bricks: he had manipulated himself as well. He had been duped by his own thinking *his entire life*. There had been no room for creativity in this, no room for true spontaneity, for being authentic or real. Something in him burst open and he began to cry again. It was not sadness that he was feeling, just a sense of release; it was as if he was throwing up his mind, all the thoughts of a lifetime were being projectile vomited out of him.

He saw himself manipulating his parents into buying him his bike. He saw how he had manipulated himself to be the slick, arrogant and smooth son of a bitch he had become. He saw that every thought, deed and action had been designed, completely and intricately *designed* for an agenda, a plan, an intention, a purpose. This had not just been in part of his life, he could see that pretty much 98% of the time he had been operating like that.

The tears kept coming and with them came more of these moments, these flashbacks of his life, things he hadn't thought about in years, things he would have never remembered otherwise, it was an avalanche now, he almost felt paralyzed to simply be a witness to this rushing onslaught of images, sights, and sounds. He did not like what he saw and felt. None of it. He really did not like the person he was seeing: calculating, self-centered, arrogant. It was like some alien being, this was not him, it couldn't be. With this thought, another feeling altogether showed up: he actually began to feel compassion for that guy, not really sorry or anything like that, just compassion. It was as though he knew that this guy had done what he needed to do because it made sense to him and he hadn't known any better. But who was feeling this? Was this him as well? But if this was him feeling this about this other guy, who was the other guy?

"That would be your ego." The bird snuck back in his consciousness with an incredible kindness and reassurance in its voice. His crying had slowed and he was wiping rivers of snot and tears off his entire face. He calmed down and looked at the bird.

"Tell me more about that, please." He found himself hoping for more reassurance or even a hug from the bird.

"What you are experiencing right now is called *perspective*. Remember how that occurred to you back there on the ledge just a little while ago, how perspective changes things?" He nodded; that seemed like a lifetime ago. "Well, in a way that's what this is. The guy you are being witness to right now is possible for you to see because of a sudden onset of perspective. You are seeing yourself from the vantage point of your Self. That Self is the energy that animated your grandfather when it inhabited 'his' body, it is the intuitive voice that has spoken to you throughout your life at different times. Sometimes you heard and ignored it, sometimes you listened, and most of the time you couldn't hear it altogether because of your focus on yourself. During this time called your life, and before and after what you call 'your' life, this Self is the animating energy that lets you be yourself, and—this is the ultimate irony—the ego only sees its own grandness and denies the very existence of the Self that makes it possible." This time the bird laughed, and the sound of it was surprisingly low and masculine.

"So who am I then?"

"You are a spiritual being having a human expe-

33

rience my friend, and that's been said before many times in many ways."

He had heard that before, had read it in the books he had consumed on spirituality. How could he have read so much, studied it so diligently, and still have been such an unbelievable asshole? He had more flashbacks of how he had treated, hell *mis*treated people all his life; even with people who had trusted him with their lives, his first concern had always been him. It really was sick, but now not in a judgmental way, more in a neutral, matter-of-fact way. He could see himself without judgment and in doing that saw how he had judged himself and the whole world constantly. Everything had to fit in a category of some kind. How exhausting that had been, he realized now. The one realizing this was calm, peaceful, and most of all, completely full of compassion for others. But who was this?

"It is your true Self. And the feeling you are having is called love. Not the conditional *idea* of love that you have had thus far in your life, but the real deal." It paused and sat down right in front of his crossed legs and looked intently at him. "I really wish for you that you choose to stay with this feeling you're in right now. You have studied everything in your life up to this point, you have used that intelligence most of the time to figure things out, to conceptualize everything, to be able to talk about it and think about it," it took in a deep pigeon-size breath, "but you never *experienced* it, because the two are exclusive of each other."

* * *

So he had never experienced all the things he had been able to talk about so well? The bird shook its little head.

"You're telling me that all the reading was point-less, because it never got me to actually experience any of it?"

"Not at all, nothing is ever pointless. But you are correct in describing the simple fact of life that theory is one thing, and actuality another. You can read all you want about falling in love, and what it feels like to desire that other person with all your heart and soul, how your life lightens when you are in love, how that feeling changes over time, deepens; how that other person becomes part of your life, part of you, while so clearly being themselves at the same time, someone you honor and love and are mystified by day after day, and for years your love changes and changes and is a neverending experience of a feeling so impersonal and yet so intimate that it cannot be truly shared with anyone else and still is for all to have if they *choose* to have it—but that is not the

35

actuality of the feeling."

"Shit, you know a lot about love for a bird." And right after he said it, he regretted it. He was missing the point, though he knew he wasn't, he had understood, at least somewhat, what the bird was saying, so why did he have to crack such an insensitive joke?

"Habit," said the bird. "Don't worry, as I mentioned before, I am not really a bird. I may tell you more about that later, we'll see." With that it lifted up one of its feet and wildly scratched the side of its head. Amazing how flexible these things were; if a person could do that, it would be hilarious.

"So you're saying that I have spent my life perfecting the art of conceptualization and intellect, but never the art of experience?" "Yes, though there certainly have been experiences in your life, plenty of them. However most were experiences of your thoughts, not of the feeling before the thought."

He shook his head; he was really trying to get this.

"Don't. Don't try to get this. That's what we are talking about. The second you try to 'get' something it's already gone. You can only *be* the experience, you can't think it, that's just the carbon copy in a way. You have been in love before, right?"

"To be honest, right now I am not sure."

"Rhetorical question, Densemeister. I know that you have. Remember Rachel?"

Oh my God, yes. He had been around 20 or so, this was a girl he had met in college and he had fallen for her so badly and madly that it had been beyond words. He ended up with a GPA of 2.5 that semester because school and classes and friends and family and life in general outside of Rachel had not mattered. It was as though the two of them had been suspended in their own world, their own universe. He had adored her. There was never any guesswork with her, because she would tell you what was going on always, and always in such an honest and authentic way, in a way that was so entirely disarming that you had to love her. And he in turn had felt loved by her, that was it, he had *felt* it, not thought about it in any way, just felt it. He had felt safe around her and would let his guard down, he didn't have to think about himself when she was around. It had been great, until he fucked it up, which he could see clearly now, sitting on this rooftop, more than a decade later.

Rachel never changed when she was with him, she had always been *real,* one hundred percent real with him and with all others. Then one day she had scared him, no, shook him to his core. She told him that she saw a huge discrepancy between how he was with her and how he was at *all other times*. She told him how she was not going to be with him if he could not be his true self in all aspects of his life, because she would not be with a liar, someone unable to be authentic in all aspects of his life, someone who was fake. He was back in the dorm room now, feeling the sting of her words, the desperate fear that was creeping into this love space that he had held for her, for them. He could see now how at that moment, he knew that she had found him out, that there was no hiding from her, and that he had to run, to turn away and run towards his arrogant and manipulative self to save him from this situation. He had unpacked the little box of information about her that he had kept in a safe place for just this moment, and attacked her. Relentlessly. He tore her apart and pulled out all the stops, making sure she understood how wrong she was, how crazy, how hopelessly romantic and naïve, and she listened quietly. Then she got up from his bed, gave him a kiss on his forehead, and said "I am so sorry" and walked out of the room. He didn't know who or what she was sorry about, his mind had been reeling at that moment, and now he could see that he shut that question down and had reassured himself that she had not turned him, that he was still who he knew he was, and that everything he had experienced with her had simply been a crush, a momentary lapse of reason, and it was time to get back to the business of living. She switched schools very shortly after and he never saw her again. Wow.

"Do you know what she was asking you to do?" the bird entered his mind inquisitively.

"To be someone I wasn't, I guess." The emotion of that night was still echoing in him. "In a way she saw something I couldn't really see in myself right then, I am not sure what that was, though I feel like I am beginning to get an idea ... " He looked around the rooftop thinking how unlikely a situation this had been so far. "I think she was telling me to change or take a hike."

"That's right." The bird had been walking back and forth and stopped thoughtfully in its tracks. "She was asking you to die, my friend."

He heard the words the bird was communicating and in the recesses of his mind there was something forming, something that would let him understand what it meant, but he couldn't get a hold of it quite yet. Rachel wanted him to die? That statement made no sense. If she had loved him—as he was sure she had—why would she have wanted him to die? He felt another stirring, the onset of another idea, another notion, an explanation, an understanding of what they were talking about here.

"That is precisely what is happening. You are gaining a deeper understanding, and that comes with perspective; it's sort of a package deal if you will," explained the bird, who was looking at him with encouragement. It was such a strange experience to look into the eyes of a pigeon and *see* something there almost human. That was not it, though … it was intelligence. "Consciousness," the bird added matter-of-factly.

"So what I am feeling inside here, this oncoming idea or perspective, or whatever you want to call it, where is it coming from and why haven't I been able to access it before?"

"For this I have to go into a little more detail. Do you have some time, my friend?" The bird grinned, and yet he knew that was impossible. He stretched out his arms in mock exasperation and settled in.

* * *

"Ego is the short answer," the bird began, walking back and forth slowly, as though in deep concentration; if it had had arms they would have been clasped behind its back. "What I call ego you may call whatever you choose, but for the time being let's say that I am talking about the idea or story of you when I say ego. This idea is something that all self-conscious beings form at one point in their experience of life, otherwise they couldn't have the experience—it's basically a universal law. This ego then produces the illusion of separateness, the idea of differentiation between 'I' and the 'other,' whatever that may be, a person or thing or circumstance, it doesn't matter." The bird stopped walking and looked at him. "With me so far?"

"Yes, I think so."

"Good. Now, as I mentioned, this ego is really a story, it is the collected history of you, the events that have occurred in what your separate self calls its life. This collection of stories, also called memories, really serve a very practical purpose in many ways. They allow you to remember language, for example, how to get dressed and other practical matters. This is the ego's design: to give you the ability to have a human experience."

"Yeah, well, that's great, but what does that have to do with Rachel wanting me to die?"

"You might want to consider turning off that incessant thought machine of yours and actually *listen*, my friend." It winked at him. "Most of you humans went ahead and misused this perfect design, because you have a choice in the matter, and turned your experiences into stories about you and who you were; you *became* them. That's when it can get messy, and ego becomes a burden. Suddenly everything has to have a meaning of some kind and has to be labeled to fit your story, and through this process you create that frail idea of 'you' that stands on its own and is in constant *need* of something." It looked straight at him. "And you, my friend, created an ego so massive and intricate that it took over every aspect of you, with barely any room for your real Self to partici- pate in your story, except for very brief moments and flashes of insight or intuition, that inner voice you had heard about, for which your ego immediately would take credit."

The bird shook its head and tucked its legs under its feathers. "When you met Rachel and fell in love the way you did, you forgot your story, you became *pres- ent*. There was no history, no hiding, no games, which is why it felt so good and your love was so full. But you allowed only this small part of your life to be free of your story, the rest of it went on as usual, and Ra- chel, a person like an eternal blank canvas, someone who lived almost entirely in the present moment at all times, saw this disharmony playing out in front of her. She knew that you either had to see this for yourself and stop doing it, or she would not be with you. When she confronted you like that, she confronted your story or ego and told it that it wasn't who you were, and that it had to in fact die in order for her to be with you. And

42

she knew that this choice was yours."

"So you're saying that this massive ego of mine, this encyclopedia called my life, was what was standing in the way of my being with her?" The bird nodded curtly. "And that I had to choose between that story and whatever that other Self was, the one in love with her?"

"Basically, yes."

"So if this ego or story is a choice I make, then I can choose that anytime, anyplace, correct? And by choosing whatever else, my ego dies?"

"In a way, yes. Only it is important to remember here that you are not that ego, it is simply an aspect of you, a means of experiencing this human life, but when you think you are the story, then it has to 'die,' because you think of it as actually you, which in truth you never have been and never will be."

This explained the way he had seen his manipulative self earlier, as though it were a person, but not him exactly. It had been the keeper of his story, of all these ideas that he had made up over the years about who he was, and what that meant, and man, had he been attached to that story. He had made people suffer for it, but most importantly he had made himself suffer for it, and he could recall all those times that he had berated himself in his own mind: you can do better than that, they don't like you, try harder, look

43

better, sound smarter, be cooler, earn more … it had never stopped, not once. His ego had made him choose it over Rachel, choose it over his friends, choose it over his joy, choose it over everything else, the ultimate ego maniac. He saw how insane he had been, and how much he had no clue who he was without his story.

Now he realized that in the past weeks, the foundations of his story—his girlfriend leaving, his business dissolving—had evaporated. He was left with nothing, nothing to use to define himself any longer, and jumping off the roof was the ultimate price his ego was asking him to pay; if it couldn't exist any longer and run the show, it was time to call it quits.

Except that he hadn't. Something or someone had stopped him and here he was. For the first time in his life, he was peaceful at that moment and realized that it was quiet and knew that he didn't need anything but to be on this rooftop and breathe.

His stomach suddenly brought him back to the moment. He hadn't eaten a thing today. Shit, he didn't think he had to—after all, suicide had been the only activity planned for the day. He had left his apartment in the morning and headed straight to his old office building to which he still had access, since the lease wasn't up for another three days. And now he was sitting here in this very surreal situation he could have never made up in his strained mind, and the reality of his body's request was hitting him. He had no idea what time it was, but the sun was higher in the sky and the air was getting nice and warm. For just a moment he considered jumping instead of getting food, but just for a brief moment—then he had to laugh as he realized that most of his life he had wished his body could just function without food.

"May we take a little break here?" he asked the bird. "I need to find something to eat."

"Yes, of course we can." And before he could even think to ask the question, the bird added: "No, I won't go anywhere."

"Great, thanks." He decided to simply go down to his office floor to check out the fridge in the kitchen; people usually left things in there. He started heading towards the door, when he thought of something and turned around.

"Can I get you anything as well?" he asked the bird.

"Yes, thanks for asking, I would really like a nice green salad with a mustard vinaigrette and a Filet Mignon." He looked at the bird not knowing what to make of that. It laughed. "Unless you can muster up some bread or seeds, I'll be fine, thanks." And shaking its head walked away from him.

* * *

flying leap

As he made his way down to the office, he noticed that things looked different, felt different, the elevator, the smell of the building. Once he reached his floor he realized that he had never really seen the carpeting or what the reception desk actually looked like, not that he hadn't looked at them before, he just never had consciously. That was an expression he and many around him had often used, not having done something "consciously." It suddenly had a whole new meaning. He could see that every time he had used that phrase he had been telling the truth in more ways than he had known possible. He had been unconscious a lot, focused only on his own mind and its incessant thought machine, missing a lot of things right in front of his eyes. And just as this thought was going through his head, he ran into a glass door and just about broke his nose.

"Fuck me!" he screamed, holding his nose. He opened the door and walked down the same hall he had walked down thousands of times before. The hall was more of an aisle framed on one side by offices for management and on the other side by cubicles. He stopped in his tracks and looked around the quiet space that had been his home for the past three years; in his mind's eye he saw everyone in their spaces, working away, the sound of busyness all around, the muted phone conversations people would have to protect their privacy, the laughter of employees standing over the edges of their wall separations as they shared a joke, and he was sad again that it was over, that it was no longer there, that his life had turned out the way that it had. His fear and loathing that had been with him for the past few weeks made him feel sick to his stomach. What was he doing here? He should get back upstairs and see it through, jump and be done with it.

But then he noticed. He noticed that he was *thinking* it, all of it. He was standing there in the office and was thinking all the shit he was thinking and it was making him feel miserable and loathsome and most of all—this was a really wild perspective—self-centered. All this crap in his mind about how bad things were, how the world was against him and all that yaddayaddayadda was bullshit and it was all about *him*. He saw himself thinking and he saw that he was doing it *at that moment* and that this shitstorm of a story he had made up to jump was entirely based on the story he had made up about himself, and that story wasn't real anymore because he wasn't willing to believe it any longer. Actually, he wasn't *interested* in this story anymore.

And with that insight came a wind—no, not literally of course, he was in an office—but it felt like a wind blowing through his mind and it was blowing

47

all those thoughts aside and left him feeling clean and light. He was done with this line of thinking, this unconscious, self-centered bullshit thought blender. It was tiring and it was useless. God, he had been such an asshole, it really sank in this time, a huge, arrogant asshole to himself and the world. He did his body shake and continued towards the kitchen, whistling.

He found some old ciabatta sandwiches, dug up a few quarters and got a soda from the machine. Walking back towards the elevator he felt as though he was closing that office door for the last time and that everything from now on was going to be different. And that was good. And scary. But mostly good.

* * *

When he got to the rooftop he felt excited to tell his new friend about his insight, and this surprised him, not that he wanted to tell it, but that he thought of the bird as his friend. How strange, to have a feeling like that towards a bird; but then he remembered how he had taken care of a friend's dog for a while, and how he had bonded with the animal, walked it three times a day, talked to it and trained it, had an actual relationship with it. Whenever he would talk to it, he imagined the dog's answer, sort of tried to figure out a "dog spin" version of his issues. It had been as though the dog were giving him advice, though he always knew that it was just him talking to himself.

He reached his spot at the ledge on the roof, and realized he still was not a hundred percent sure that he was done with the whole jumping idea yet; after all, nothing had actually changed.

"Oh really?" asked the bird as it landed on his head.

"Holy crap! Stop doing that, you're going to give me a heart attack for Chrissakes!"

"Well, that way at least you don't have to jump," chuckled the bird. "So, did you get me something to eat?" He waved his hand above his head to get the bird to fly off, and it landed on his shoulder.

"I ... it ... well, I've got some sandwiches, I could pull some pieces off for you." He felt a tinge of guilt because frankly, he had neglected to consider the bird's hunger altogether.

"I'm kidding, your Holy Denseness, I know what you brought, and I know that you forgot about me, but most of all, I am curious about your journey into your old world." The bird pecked at his ear gingerly.

"Hey, stop that, and stop reading my mind, it's getting annoying, and is moving into major creepiness territory! It's really none of your business what goes on in my mind, you know ... " he said without

49

real conviction. He did feel a little creeped out but at the same time was comforted that someone else was there, someone to share his insights and listen in this completely neutral way, but yet in a way that felt warm and caring, even if it was a bird.

The pigeon flew off his shoulder and parked itself in front of him. "So, anyway, your insights down below were interesting, this whole business about seeing yourself think and for the first time really *seeing* your story."

"Vat du u mean, ven you scay 'sceeing' like that?" he asked with his mouth full of sandwich.

The bird looked at him like a disapproving mother. "I mean that you actually experienced it, you felt it, you saw it. It wasn't some concept or idea, it was real. That makes all the difference." It plopped itself down as though to nest eggs. "You have spent most of your life in theory; it was never a life that was real, really. You spent your time perfecting the art of faking your life, like most people actually do, and what I mean by that is that you never understood that you were *creating* everything you called your life, all of it, all of the time. You read books about it, thought about it, talked about it, and did all this very well—as a matter of fact you were blessed, or in this case, cursed, with a good intellect, and that made you perfect at it." The bird tilted its head. "All the theory in the world doesn't cut

50

it, when it comes to living a life. As I mentioned earlier, everyone is in the same boat, everyone is making up their story as they go along, the key to actually *living* your life rather than watching your life, is understanding this difference and *seeing* it."

"So you're saying that my life up to this point wasn't real, because I was making up my story but didn't know that I was?"

"In a way, yes, but also no. Everything is real, but it depends on how aware you are of the process that makes it real." The bird hesitated, and then perked up. "I just remembered something that might help you see what we're talking about here; do you remember that funny saying your friend Ben told you last summer when you were driving to see friends in the Hamptons?"

This was getting freakier by the moment. What was the bird talking about now? How did it know such details from his life? And what about Ben? He didn't remember having any friends in the Hamptons ... but now it was coming back; they hadn't gone to see friends, they had gone to see investors who were going to fund Ben's business; Ben had offered to introduce him to them. He had met Ben only two years earlier at a conference and they had become friends. They had a lot in common, though Ben always made sure to mention that he had gone to Har-

51

vard, as though that were some badge of honor, made him just that much more special, and he had enjoyed the competition that they had quietly understood to have entered into with each other. He was always going to be the one who had only gone to a private liberal arts college in the Midwest, but he had gotten himself a Master's Degree as well, which Ben hadn't and so they were constantly battling over the value of a Harvard BA versus having a Master's, but Ben always pulled out his trump card, that he *could* still get a Master's, but the chances of *his* ever going to Harvard, well, they were ...

And then he noticed he was vomiting his mind out again; this was like a disease. What had the bird asked about again? Something about a saying Ben had told him. What was it? Oh yes: "There are three types of people in this world: the ones who make things happen, the ones who watch things happen, and the ones who say 'What the fuck just happened?' "

"Yes, that one," the bird said. "Now, even though most people will think of themselves as part of one of those groups, by far the biggest number will actually be in a fourth group, the ones who say 'There are things, and they are happening.' " The bird paused for a moment and then looked at him directly with those black eyes.

"See, the truth of the matter is, *there are no*

things," it said intensely. "The only *thing* there is, is no-thing and yet it is the most real some-thing can ever be."

Silence.

"Well, what is *it*?" He felt like he was in some bad Hollywood version of a spiritual-teacher-meets-eager-student parable.

"You. The real you, the one who is having this experience called your life, the one who speaks to you in those moments that are either quiet enough so you can hear it, or crazy enough that it sticks out with its quiet reassurance among the maelstrom of your thinking. The one who loves, the one who knows, the one who is without fear, without judgment, the one who simply is there, behind the curtain."

At that he stopped chewing and his mind went into some kind of funky overdrive. Images of his life, no, his story, started flying through his head, except at this moment he was watching it from a distance, he was looking at it like a movie, and it all made sense. Everything made sense. As he sat there watching his mind reel, he realized he had been the director, the producer, the actor, and most importantly, the writer of this story. It wasn't that there was something going on—something was behind the curtain, he had been behind the curtain all along, so engrossed in what he had been making up

53

that he had forgotten himself completely. But what the hell did that *mean*? He was having thoughts he had never had before and though he felt fine, hell, he actually felt great, he also felt completely clueless. What the hell was going on with him?

"You are at your funeral and waking up, my friend," the bird said.

* * *

At that he swallowed a piece of sandwich that had been sitting in his half-open mouth for the past couple of minutes, took a swig of the nasty sugary drink posing as a natural fruit juice and stared at the bird with a mixture of wonder, utter disbelief, trepidation, and excitement. What does one say to that? It was as though his brain was melting, it couldn't come up with anything for him to say, anything for him to *think*. If he had wondered about the meaning of it all before, and by this he meant his definition of meaning earlier that day, and how things didn't have one anymore and that was the reason why he was going to end his meaningless existence, then this beat all that by lengths. There was nothing he could come up with in his mind, as though it were running on empty. Maybe he was truly insane now, and this is what it felt like.

The bird started to laugh. "You are not going crazy my friend, don't worry; as a matter of fact, you are having the experience of a lucid mind for the first time in your life." It got up and started swinging its head back and forth. "You are, however, in the process of losing your mind; it just happens completely differently from the way people typically think of it. Losing one's mind in a healthy way is what you are doing, and what popular belief out there has come to judge as insanity is an entirely different and unhealthy way to lose one's mind." It flew up on the ledge next to him. "Just to be clear."

He rubbed his temples to get some sense back in his head and remembered how he used to always laugh at actors in movies rubbing their temples because it seemed such a ludicrous and unrealistic act—pun intended—and yet here he was. And it helped. Who knew?

"Okeydokey, so I gather from what you said, and from the fact that I am sitting here and feeling the distinctive oncoming aftermath of the meal in my stomach, that I am still here and I am still *with* this body. That I am, at least in the popular cultural definition, *not* dead. Right?" He looked the bird in the eyes, trying to appear assured, but failed miserably.

"No, you're not. Not by popular cultural definition." It winked.

"So in what way *am* I dead? Are you just messing

with me? I need some answers here."

"Well, need in general is not a good idea, but I'll let that one go. I'm sure we'll get to that later, and answers you shall receive, plenty of them. Let me start by going back to that earlier question of your death, and what death means to you." It paused for a moment as though to make sure he understood, and he did.

"Good. Now, you were stuck on that whole notion of death being connected entirely to your body dying, or to your 'physical and psychological existence' as you had said earlier. That is only one definition of dying, and a very limited one I might add." With that it plopped down on the ledge and had a very satisfied look on its face.

"Okay … aaaand?" he queried.

The bird just shook its head. He imagined that it would have pursed its lips just then if it had had any. "See, dying is going on all the time, in limitless ways. I usually don't use that word because it has so much emotion and fear attached for you, but the process is still the same." It thought for a moment. "Things are coming and going all the time, but beyond that, thoughts are coming and going all the time. Where are they before you are aware of them? Where do they go after you have finished them? Have you any idea, have you ever asked yourself that?"

No, he hadn't, and that was one strange and tickling question to consider. He now found himself back
as a barely teenage boy when he and a friend had
become involved with the local planetarium and they
had learned everything there was to learn about as-
tronomy, the galaxy, the stars, and the universe. At
first it had been all about learning the facts, but then
it became a different experience; he and his buddy
became members in the astronomers' club which ran
the observatory and were awarded the task of setting
up the huge telescope for groups coming through on
Tuesday nights. They would point the thing at Sat-
urn and Jupiter and some galaxy or nebula that was
visible from Earth, and people would look through
it and stand in awe. As did he. He and his friend
would spend hours during the summer laying in the
grass at night staring at the endless sky, not saying much, just exploring the depth of the stars, more
with their minds than with their eyes really. And
in those moments, the fact that they were looking
at the past and that space had no end or beginning
would float around his head; in those moments his
mind felt tickled. It was as though he were reach-
ing the limit of his mind, he was bumping into some
kind of invisible wall of reasoning that he was not to
cross, and it was then that he considered for the first
time that nothing was as it seemed, that there was

more, far more, going on than his feeble mind could ever grasp. It had felt good.

"That is a wonderful feeling," said the bird in agreement. "And you have been chasing it all your life. So where have those thoughts you just pulled up, called a memory, been since you had them last? Were you just back there in that field? Have you been there all along, wondering and searching, bumping into that wall of yours? How is a thought you are having about the past different from a thought about the future or the present moment?"

It flapped its wings briefly. "A thought is a thought is a thought, my friend. They come and go, but you are not-your-thoughts, you are the thinker. Reflect on that. A thought is always attached to the idea of *time*, it has to, for without a point of reference it can't exist. A thought creates the idea of distinction. This and the other. If you can't think that you are distinctively you, then how would you know what anything else is? Thinking is useful, don't get me wrong, but it is so important to be aware of thought *existing*. It is the tool your Being uses to experience the You as a *human* being. Without thought there would be no experience of you. And you choose every thought you have at any moment in your life. Most choose the same thoughts over and over again and create this sense of permanence around what you call your life.

Then these thoughts become you and you forget that you are in fact still choosing your thoughts, again and again, moment to moment. They are not there fixed inside yourself, though it may seem that way at times, they come and go constantly. What and how you choose to think at any moment creates the experience you are having as a human. So if you choose different thoughts, what happens to the other ones? What happens to the 'you' you thought you were?"

Jesus, that bird was coming at him from all directions. If he couldn't even be sure of a thought being his, whose was it then? And since thoughts did come and go, what could he then count on? Anything? If he couldn't even trust his own thinking any longer, could he trust himself? And if his thinking was coming and going all the time, and he was just a story made up of thoughts, his thoughts, then what or who was he? A thought? An idea? Just a story? And if that story was ending now, if he had actually decided to no longer be the story he had been for so long, a story he really wasn't interested in anymore, shit, a story he didn't really *like*, then what was left? Who was sitting here on the rooftop talking to a bird?

At that moment he noticed his breathing had grown agitated and his heart was racing and it brought him out of his mind back to right then, and he felt that comfortable emptiness again, that tickling of his mind gently in the background, and he realized that who he had been was no longer there. There were ideas and memories there, but they weren't him. And then it hit him: it was as though he had died and he was simply looking at the memory of who he had been, not the actual man. Strange. And somehow liberating. And scary as shit. And really, really strange.

* * *

All of this made sense and felt right, he knew that and he knew it with total certainty. It was a different kind of certainty though. Not the way he had felt certain before in his life, when certainty had to do with knowing the facts, communicating them effectively, and convincing others that those facts were correct. Being able to do that without any doubt had been certainty. Then there had been the many times where he simply had made shit up just to look certain. Or he would play the situation in such a way that he could position himself in alignment with the one who looked the most certain, making him look certain as well. But none of that had ever come close to the certainty he felt right then about whom he was *not* any longer, that this someone had in fact died.

Except he hadn't. There was this someone who had died and then there was this someone who hadn't, the someone who was thinking this right now. But before he could put this into words, the bird hopped off the ledge and parked itself on his right knee.

"That is interesting, isn't it? Who or what *is* aware of what you used to be, of the person, the story that now lies in front of you dying?" It nodded its little head as if contemplating the answer to that question for the very first time, though he had a feeling it wasn't. The bird snickered at that.

"You're right, it's not the first time. But every single time it's different and new. Right now, in your case, you are in the midst of letting the ego self, or the story, go. It's not gone yet, as a matter of fact it probably will take a while longer to be gone completely, but you are at the funeral and are now entering into a different phase, a phase of waking up to your Self, the Self that I mentioned earlier."

"So are you saying there are two of me?" This was even more confusing, but then again, confusion was quickly becoming his middle name.

"Funny. And no, there are not two of you; there are, however, different *aspects* of you. These different aspects show themselves in limitless ways, but for what's important here right now let's just say that there is your real Self and the little self—the story. The first one is the real McCoy, the other one is an individuated expression of the Self, and that

61

individuated expression in your case is called a human being." It hopped onto his other knee. "It is very simple and elegant, really. You create this idea of an individuated self that thinks of itself as separate from everything else and then get to make up whatever you choose in the process. That is the story. But that's also all it is, just a story. Now, you also get all these wonderful tools to play with in order to make this story *real* to you. You get the five senses, a body, thought and memory to remember it all, emotions to experience your thinking and its effects, and all of that in a three dimensional world that you seem to be a part of, but yet strangely are separated from as well." Silence. "It's quite the show you get to put on for yourselves."

This was not new to him as a concept, he had read something like that before. But as he was listening now, it felt real to him, it was as though the concepts had come to life and he was in the middle of it. He could actually *see* this individuated self that he had created, in all its glory and ugly detail, the whole story was laid out right in front of him. And even though he knew that this had been him until just very recently, the memories of his life were quickly becoming less personal, almost as though they could be someone else's.

While he was feeling and seeing this, he was also

experiencing a sense of deep and relaxing calm, in a way he never had before. It reminded him of how he used to feel as a small child when something had scared him in his dreams and his mother came and simply held him, reassuring him that it had been just a dream and that all was well and he was safe. There was such incredible warmth, an embrace like that was what he was feeling now, except bigger in a way—but that wasn't it, either.

And he noticed then that he was crying again, except this time they were tears of a deep joy with the realization that he was not alone, that he had never been alone, but that he had felt that way all his life, abandoned and left to his own devices to make the best of it all. God, how hard that had been. Underneath the know-it-all, popular, go-getter, arrogant, and oh-so-charming life story had been that nagging feeling of being completely and utterly on his own. This felt so different and so much better.

"The second you try to put words or thoughts to it, the experience simply becomes an idea or concept, and that's what you did all your life with any real feelings you ever had. Look where that got you." It poked him in the knee with its beak.

"The only thing that matters is that you are *seeing* this, as you so aptly put it. This seeing is what happens when you wake up from your dream or the story you used to see as your life. This can be painful and shocking at first,"—*no shit*, he thought—"but very quickly your Self steps into that space and reassures you that all is well. This is the calm you are feeling. And the perspective you now have on your story is a nice side effect. In a way it's fun, because you still get to have all the memories you choose, but they look different and can serve a different purpose."

Right then he remembered a quote that he had always enjoyed: "Life is but a dream within a dream," or something like that. Kind of a sick man Poe was, really; if he had thought that, why on earth would he write such nightmarish stories? Nonetheless there was truth in that line. His story had been a sort of dream, because when had it ever been real? All the trials and tribulations he had been through, the horrors of being a teenager, learning the rules of the game and becoming a good player, always on the lookout for the next challenge or danger. And of course all the triumphs as well. He had had a good run until recently when all had gone to hell, but with this new vantage point he found himself with the question of whether any of it had been real. What was ever real? Was this right now real? Was he having this conversation? Had he maybe already jumped and was going through some kind of life review process with angel bird by his side? How could he know that all these memories of "his" life were real, had actually ever been real, and that they had even been his at all?

"You can't," said the bird.

* * *

He looked at the bird with some serious fault lines across his forehead. "Are you telling me that I have had this whole life, and memories to prove it, and I pretty much liked that life, well, I had no reason to change it anyway, and most of all I felt pretty sure of myself and knew what was real and what wasn't. At least I believed that I had some certainty, some clue about what my life meant, what it was, who I was. And now you're telling me that I can't be sure about anything anymore? What kind of trade is that?" He was getting pissed off. "Shit, at least my life made sense, I could tell real from fiction, I knew who I was, what I was! Now I sit here and you make me feel all peaceful and wonderful inside and that puts me on a track to nowhere land. I don't know that I would want that! I don't know if that is a life worth living! This is bullshit, you are full of it and all this is some trip I am on and I don't like it or want it. If I can't have my life back, and the only other choice is to live in this place of peace but have no clue what is real anymore, well, Sir, I choose death!"

He knew the last line was a bit melodramatic.

65

flying leap

"May I point something out here?" the bird asked calmly.

He nodded. This had better be good.

"The one who is doing the complaining here is the very one who wants you to go back to the life you just described. The one who tried everything to make that happen again; the one who plodded and pleaded and manipulated you to regain some semblance of control over your life and its circumstances; the one who in the end couldn't do it, couldn't pull off the ultimate con of humanity, to make you believe that you *are* your thoughts, and that these thoughts are a factual reality that you are subject to; the one who ended up on this rooftop with its last measure of control, the decision to 'end it all' and jump. This is the one who just reared its head with what it has left in its struggle, telling you and itself that control is the measure of a certain life, that knowing what is real is the test of your existence. Without knowing what is real and what is not, how are you to exist, it asks; and by asking, utilizes the oldest trick in the book of human experience: fear."

He sat there for a moment, a bit shocked at the intensity with which the bird had communicated this, though without aggression, judgment, or arrogance. All the times in his life when he had been in an intense situation, there had always been a very strong energy in the room. An energy of superiority, though this was not limited to the physical exchange. No, he had been in many intense battles of words, and they all had been marked by another element ... what was it ... his mind was trying to identify it ... almost could see it, the same way a word could be on the tip of his tongue. And then it popped into his mind: violence. He wasn't sure what that meant exactly, but he knew that it was missing in the bird.

"The basis of all egoic activity is based in fear, and all fear is, in one form or another, violent. Now, to be sure, this does not refer to the limited idea of violence you may have subscribed to thus far, but to a larger context of fear. It truly is the biggest lie of them all. It is in its nature violent, because it is based on the erroneous assumption that you are alone, a separate being that is looking for meaning and connection in this world that you have created with your thoughts, and that is one fearful existence. Why do you think babies cry when they first arrive? They suddenly find themselves naked in this world that they are not separate from, and they feel the fear that is all around." The bird stood and stretched its wings. "Believe me, when you're not prepared for that, it's a shocker."

But how is that related to not being able to tell what is real and what is not? he wondered.

"Have you been listening at all?"

flying leap

Maybe he hadn't. He felt like standing up to stretch his body and walked around in circles. That usually had helped him clear his mind. Was he missing something? Words and images were flying through his mind: fear, violence, intensity, the bird's reaction to his outburst, the way he had felt right before then, how he felt now. No, nothing was coming to his mind. He looked up at the sky and the sun, and noticed the sound of the slight breeze in his ears and how it moved his hair. He smelled the familiar scents of the city: warm concrete, car exhaust, and a gentle floral aroma from the budding trees below.

"That is the only thing I know. That I am here, right now. I am certain of that, because I can feel it. And I know that I am thinking that right now, but I also know that I felt that before I told you this or even thought it. It's the same way I knew that I loved Rachel. *That* is for certain, *that* is real, and it feels good." He looked at the bird. "See, I was listening." And he gave the bird his finest shit grin.

"You really do know how to put on an act, don't you?" the bird noted. "The point you were making to yourself earlier was simply a realization, you understood the nature of thought and saw the role it made you play in your own life and how that was a simple fact. Everything is thought, and you are the thinker, not the thought. Your life was a testament to a life lived in the fake certainty that arises out of believing that you are your thoughts, repeating similar thoughts and thought patterns over and over again, until they become so automatic that there is nothing else, just the same thoughts, giving you this sense of permanence and of who you think you are."

"Okay, so how does this all fit together, what does it actually *mean*?" He shrugged his shoulders in mock exasperation. "I mean, fuck, this morning everything at least made sense and I was pretty sure that dying was going to solve all my issues. Now I can see how that won't solve anything, but I am not sure where that leaves me."

"Great point, actually: where does that 'leave you'? In a way you are leaving; you are leaving behind the thoughts of old, the ideas and story that have been you for so long, and in its place you are left with no-thing. That's the point, my friend."

"I am left with no-thing. It feels so weird to hear that."

"As I told you in the beginning, welcome to weirdness. Except what might feel weird to you now is actually the real normal, the real sane. You have been conned by your own mind as billions of humans are, nothing unusual going on here. But you chose to listen when you did, you heard me, and thus you died in a way that you never expected, though die you had to, and now you get to choose again and again what your next move, idea or creation shall be, but for one."

"And that would be ... ?"

"Wait for it, wait for it ... " Man, that bird had a taste for drama. "To go back to the life you had."

"Well, that's a relief, since it wasn't working anyway. But what am I going to do with this choice thing? I mean, I get that we make choices, but you make it sound as though it's a really big deal."

The bird sneezed, or at least it looked and sounded like a sneeze, he wasn't sure. "Gesundheit."

It shook its head as though it were trying to get something out. "Better. So where were we? Ah, yes, the idea of choice. It is actually more integral to life than you have ever imagined. Without choice nothing exists, not you, not me, not this city, the planet, the solar system, Einstein's theory of relativity, hot dogs, cars, clouds, rocks, annoying phone menus, economies, war, poverty, wealth, hatred, suffering–"

"I get the point," he interrupted.

"Oh, but do you? I think you see choice in the very limited framework of your life circumstances, as it pertains to you and your life, the options before you, the one or the other, picking whichever makes sense."

"Well, yeah. But doesn't choice mean that there is always one and another?" How else could it work?

70

"No. That is the prevailing *idea* around choice that you and your other human siblings have made up—it goes far deeper than that." It took a deep breath. "It is correct that there is one underlying choice that had to take place for this conversation and everything else to exist, but let's talk about that later. Right now I would like to ask you to consider that there are limitless choices available at all times, and that the only difference in what choice you make is based on one thing: whether you make that choice based on fear or love."

Oh, he had so read that before, many times in fact, the idea that there were only two feelings, fear and love. That was easy. He knew not to make choices based on fear, stress, sadness … he knew to pay attention and allow for these negative emotions, thus making a better choice as a result. And when he was in a good place, his mind was clearer and he would automatically make better choices. He had that nailed.

The bird was shaking its head.

"What?"

"You have no idea what you are talking about. Actually, let me rephrase that: all you have *is* an idea."

"I am so tired of your bullshit! I know stuff. Give me some credit here."

"Really, you want credit now? For what exactly? And why would you think I could give it, much less would want to give it?" It shook its head like a disappointed father.

"Well, at least I am trying here—"

"Just stop it! Stop making it about you, and about you in the smallest way possible. That is your fear at work! There is only fear and love, but in the largest truth of it all, there is only love and nothing else. That's what choice is for!"

"I don't get it."

"Well, would you like to?"

"Yeah, I would."

The bird flew up on his shoulder and poked his ear. "Well, then get ready for the ride of your life."

f a

More like the ride *for* his life, and he knew it. They had spent most of the day on that rooftop and as the sun was going down, it became a bit chilly. They decided to go to his place and continue the conversation. They left separately, because he thought it would add to the weirdness of it all if he was walking around with a pigeon on his shoulder.

What a day it had been.

When he got back to his building, he opened the window for the bird to come in. It had been waiting on the windowsill, but at this point that had become normal, and that was weird—how could something be normal and weird at the same time? He was hungry again and decided to make soup, chopping up veggies and dicing and spicing and loving it. Making the soup was an act of anchoring; it gave him a sense of groundedness. He felt the need to position himself for what was to come; he was scared but infinitely curious. He sat down at the kitchen table where the bird was enjoying some cashews.

The bird hadn't been in his mind since they had left the rooftop, or at least that's what it felt like. Almost as though it had been imagined after all, but here it was again, in all its reality.

"Good nuts."

"I'm glad you like them."

"Are they organic?"

"Are you kidding me?"

"Yeah." The bird winked.

"I really don't know what to make of it all yet," he said. "It seems both utterly surreal and incredibly real at the same time, but I don't know what that actually means. This is so beyond description."

"Which is exactly the place to be!" The bird seemed giddy, like a kid who just received a long-awaited ice cream cone. "See, most of a human life is spent try-ing to label and define everything that goes on in the mind. Every thought has to have a definition, a meaning, or at the very least a *reason*, to exist. Now all of those only make sense to the *owner* of the thoughts"—he realized the bird would have made air quotes with its fingers had it had any—"and some-times their logic can seem extreme or radical, weak and lost, or completely crazy, at least by popular definition."

"Well, if you think about it, there have always been

people with ideas that most would have thought were crazy at the time, and then those ideas turned out to be visionary." *Much like me at times*, he thought.

At this the bird coughed up a cashew. "Goodness, I hope you heard that one! Get over yourself already. This is exactly what I am talking about, that unchecked ego that sneaks in and sets up shop to create this shadow of a real you that is all about itself and only that."

"Geez, chill out, I'm still using my training wheels here."

The bird shook its head wildly, tossing cashews in the air. "That is not the point. You have seen something today, and it has changed you. You will not go back to the way things were, so you must pay attention. You have to have vigilance and rigor! That gigantic ego of yours that you created was like a tumor that spread throughout your brain into its finest branches and affected every-aspect-of-you. So when you have thoughts like the one just then, you have to be aware and see it for what it is: a lie."

"Okay, okay, I'll pay more attention."

The bird was right and he knew it. As he listened, it had become clear to him what was going on. His whole life he had actually never been in control of his own mind. He knew that he had done all the thinking, but at the same time he now saw how it had taken on its own life or rhythm and had run on automatic pilot. Occasionally he had had an original idea but generally it had been all about his thoughts, his ideas, his importance. There had no longer been room for being, just a self-modifying and self-serving thought construct which meant that he no longer had been able to actually *live*. With that, the idea of his visionary greatness felt like something he would eat because it looked so good, and the second he swallowed it, he would know it was a mistake and pay the price. He would feel sick, want to get rid of it as fast as he could, and even thinking about the food would confirm its ill nature. He shook his body at the thought and decided to stay away from it from now on. Not just that one. All of the thoughts that tasted like this. He could do that. He *would* do that. Once and for all.

"You are catching on. Remember, you are doing this for your Self. This is not about being a good person or even a better person, this is about simply being You. If you have a thought that even remotely smells like it is about you, accept it and let it go. Don't judge it or fight it, and most importantly, don't judge yourself for having it. That's called having a human experience. But there is a big difference between the experience having you and you having the experience: in one you are the victim, and in the other you are the creator."

"How does fear play into all this?" He could see how his ego had worked, he now felt the ugliness of it, the bad-tasting heaviness of it, but how was that fear?

"Ego is fear," the bird said.

If ego was fear, then everything that his ego had ever cooked up, plotted, judged, or decided had been based in fear. But wasn't fear something you felt? He tried to remember the times he had been afraid in his life: back in school when a bully started a fight with him and he ended up with his first busted lip, when his motorcycle had slipped out from under him and he thought he wasn't going to make it, when he had lost his first job and feared that that was the end of his professional life altogether, when Rachel had left him. Even some of his "grandest" moments had been filled with the fear of "no longer" or "soon to be over." That made sense, he just couldn't quite understand it.

"You are looking at the basic nature of fear. Everything ego is fear. Period. Ego is your story, and the story is you. It is based on time. Without time, there would be no story. But because it is based in time, and time is moving in this story, you are constantly seeking ways to make your story more real, more permanent, so that *you* may be more real and permanent. But you are not. The ego knows this and thus knows that it is not real; it is the most unreal part about you, and that is a fearful place to be, to know that you are not real, and to be condemned to create evidence of your realness. The ego is born out of the illusion of time and creates the illusion of itself. And then it spends the rest of its time in this human form, trying desperately to avoid this truth. Could you be full of any more fear than that?"

That he had not thought of before. The bird surely had a way. "So if all ego is fear and I am not my ego, then who am I?"

"We'll talk about that tomorrow. I'm tired." The bird stretched its wings, hopped onto the windowsill, and turned around. "Enjoy your soup." And with that it flew off.

For a second he was afraid that it might not come back.

Funny, there it was again.

Fear.

* * *

He slept okay that night. He didn't dream so much as he experienced these weird feelings. He had had them before, but this time they were more intense and meant something else, but he didn't know what. It was clear to him in his sleep that he was not permanent, that he was basically a fluctuating energy in a physical form, and that all he had created and attached to this energy was what he knew to be himself. But since it was just an impermanent energy it also wasn't him, couldn't be him, because it wasn't solid, and the idea of himself was supposed to be somewhat solid and real. All this was quite disconcerting.

At least he didn't experience his moroseness upon waking. He couldn't remember when it had started exactly, but for a very long time he had been curious about life in a larger sense and had read all those books and watched anything on spirituality and quantum physics, and had spent considerable time on the subject. He had come to think of himself as a well-informed spiritual seeker at the very least, and in his greatest delusions of grandeur, he thought he was at least partially enlightened. That was funny now. And really arrogant.

At some point he had started to play with the notion of his own and undeniably certain death and the implications of this. So he had picked up more books on the subject, had read them and constructed his own system of logic around it all, except he never managed to put it together quite right, it never really had worked. With these ideas of impermanence had come the conundrum of what else he might be beyond this. It had been like facing an abyss. And whenever he had taken naps or had woken up in the morning, this cognitive dissonance had been right there in his mind, the inevitable and inescapable fact of his impermanence, staring at nothing, while wanting to be permanent and real. And it had felt morose. So he had started to accept his moroseness and at the same time made a deal with himself that he would find an answer to this ultimate discord, because he did not want to get all the way to his own death and still be sitting there with this question unresolved. He just had a feeling that this could be a bad thing.

Yet the morning after what had been the most bizarre day of his life on this planet, the moroseness wasn't there. Huh, almost a bit strange, like an annoying friend you got used to and then suddenly wasn't there anymore and you realized you missed him. As a matter of fact, once he had reached the end of this last thought session, he felt quiet, nothing in particular, just quiet. And no moroseness in sight. He wondered whether that meant he now had the answer to his question?

Nope, nothing there. He stretched and turned towards his nightstand to see what time it was.

"Jesus fucking Christ almighty!" He jumped almost ten feet out of bed after turning his head and having the bird's beak practically in his eye. It had been sitting right next to him for God knows how long and he had never noticed. He clutched his chest, ready for his heart to give out. What a way to go that would be after his carefully planned exit. "Don't *ever* do that again, alright? If you want me dead, you should have just let me jump yesterday." And at that he had to laugh. How divinely funny and strange this all was. He went into the kitchen to have some breakfast.

"I really did not want to interrupt your thought process. You really are just finding out what it is like to see your thinking as something separate from *you*. As you do that, different ideas start to show up and with them, different answers to the same questions you may have asked yourself for a long time." That was true. How else could the moroseness have disappeared, even though that still left him wondering who the hell he actually was.

"That depends entirely on where you are asking the question from."

"Come again?"

The bird swallowed a piece of granola that it had really been enjoying, organic. "We are not talking about a physical location here, at least not in the human sense. Perspective is the key. When you ask the question of who you are from the ego perspective, then you are your story, which means you will have a slew of thoughts and ideas that you can pull up to explain who you are. This is the time-bound version of you with a beginning and an end—"

"*Middle* and end."

"How would you ever know when your middle is?" It tilted its head.

He hadn't thought of that before.

"Thank you. So, this ego self asks who you are, and contained within the time-bound idea of beginning and end it can pretty much recite the memories and the story that explain you or define you. Within that realm you have your opinions, likes and dislikes and so on, thus making you a package deal that makes sense to itself. But it is also a very limited perspective, because it leaves out completely all the other aspects of your Self. It puts you in that separate space. Only when you see yourself as the separate entity living in a world of separateness does this 'you' make sense and work; it is also a very lonely place to be. From that perspective, it is absolutely logical that you would try to connect with other humans in any way possible, actually try to create a sense of connectedness with any parts of the world through all kinds of activities that put you in a place of *relating*. Only through relating to something else can you maintain your sense of separate self while attempting to overcome the disconnectedness that comes with it. Quite ironic, isn't it?"

Yes, it was. This really felt right and he understood what the bird was saying. Looking back at his life story—as he thought of it now—he could clearly see that very mechanism at work in him; all he had ever tried to do was make himself more real by relating to the people and circumstances around him. All this controlling and manipulating he had done had served only one purpose: to know that he existed, that he could influence things and thus make his effect on the world more real. As he recalled the many times he had functioned that way, another idea crept into his mind: all this time he had believed that he was relating with the world "out there," the people and places. But with his new perspective, he saw he had been relating only to his own thinking about people and places, nothing else. It had always been him, his ego self, that he had in fact related to. In this way he had never truly experienced another person or circumstance, only his own thoughts—except with Rachel. He now could see that he had had moments of just being with her, actually seeing her and feeling her without his own brain getting in the way, instead simply serving as a tool to be with her.

"Nicely put, my friend. That is the experience and perspective of the ego self in that smallest of ways.

From that vantage point, the very limited question of who you are is answered quite simply: 'I think, therefore I am.' "

Whoa, that made a whole lot of different sense now. He wondered if Descartes had really meant it that way.

* * *

"It changes everything, doesn't it, when all you do is expand the 'idea' of who you are. So much more comes into view, your experience deepens." The bird was thoughtfully looking out the window.

"Well, yeah, it does."

They both sat there in silence. He felt a deep kinship with the bird, how strange and yet so familiar this had become ... and yet it wasn't the bird itself, it was the conversation, the feel of it, so intimate and comfortable. It really had felt that way since the rooftop—otherwise he surely would have jumped. It seemed so odd now that this had been his solution only twenty-four hours ago. It was clear now how unclear his thinking had been, that it had made him believe that jumping was the only logical thing to do. All his thoughts had become more narrow over the past few weeks, as if to bring them to one point all along.

He had literally been on a trip, the ultimate

thought trip to (k)nowhere. He had to laugh at that, the word floating in front of his mental eye, how elegantly it described what his unaware and unchecked thinking had done; how it had sold him on the idea that it was completely in-the-know and that he had to go you-know-where with it: nowhere. But instead he had ended up now and here—now_here. One space could make all the difference.

"I am glad you are here." The bird entered his mind again with great warmth. "For a while it was a bit touch and go with you. I really wasn't sure that you were going to hear me, whether it might be too late. But here we are. It's a beautiful thing. And this feeling you find yourself in now is the real You, the real Self. As it becomes more present in you, you will be more aware of the full range of life. There is so much to experience, and when you move into your Self, it becomes available to you. This is impossible when life is lived from that other, smallest aspect of you, your separated ego story of me, me, me. This does not mean that this ego self is worthless or bad, far from it. As I said yesterday, it is not only necessary, it makes your human experience possible. But when it becomes all you see of your Self, life gets very limited in scope and at best you have moments of insight, of bliss or joy, when you get to understand that all life is a sight from within, never without."

flying leap

"But how is that practical? People still have to make a living, get along with others, relate to the world, pay the bills, put food on the table ... I love what you're saying, don't get me wrong. As a matter of fact I have been spending the biggest part of my life trying to get to this very moment, this very feeling, but this does beg the question of practicality. I mean, right at this moment I don't feel that I need anything, I am perfectly happy and content sitting here and feeling this way. But eventually I will have to go out there and face the world again, right?" Somehow as the words left his mouth he was certain that there was an answer to this, but he couldn't find it in himself.

"Well, you make a valid point, and I would venture to say that there is nothing more practical than living from, through, and entirely as your Self. See, living in this space does not mean that you cease to function or exist. That, in fact, is the very powerful lie the ego will put in place to keep you from ever being there—the fear of annihilation. The ego is the ultimate nihilist, for all it can ever create is a time-bound idea of self that is at best filled with very set and limited *ideas* about being and at worst very set and limited *beliefs* about the right way to live. As a matter of fact, that is one definition of fanaticism: to cling to a particular belief about one's place in the world, the very world that you created yourself in the first place, mind you, and to do so at your and others' peril if need be. The nihilist's ultimate fulfillment of promise is first to annihilate the 'opposing' belief and, if that doesn't work, to die defending its own."

"That's war, isn't it?"

"No, that's called the current state of humanity. And it's very *impractical*."

The bird had another bite of granola. "The ego's way is as I just described: life is hard, it's about me, me, me in one form or another. It exists in a state of separation and needs hard work and willpower to achieve anything, usually in opposition to or competition with some other, whatever that may be. This is hardly practical, it's simply hard." He nodded to that. "Being in your space of Self, on the other hand, means that you live in harmony with your story, you know that there is one, that you are making it up and that you get to make up whatever you want, at any time in any way you choose. Period. You are completely unimpeded by any ideas about what you can or cannot do, of who you are or are not. There is total freedom to choose any aspect of You and how you would like to show up in the world, moment to moment, knowing that here and now is the only reality that exists. How much more practical can it get?"

flying leap

And before he had fully formulated the thought in his mind, the bird continued: "And no, that is not irresponsible, actually it is the most responsible way to live, because rather than re-acting to the same thoughts over and over again, you are response-able; life is of your making and your creation and you get to respond to it all with full creativity and the power of the universe behind it. In my book it doesn't get any more practical than that, at least not in human form."

That was not the answer he had expected, and most certainly not whatever had been dangling in the back of his mind. As he tried to make sense of what the bird had just said, another memory popped into his mind: there he was at the age of seventeen, sitting in the car with his then girlfriend Valerie, a sweet girl who he could see now had been wise beyond her years. (Funny how this same memory had felt and thus meant something completely different the last time he had thought it.) He had figured out in his mind that he had to dump her, because she made him uncomfortable with her intensity. He had been one intense guy, but that was the intensity of the turbo-charged, hormonally-exploding, ego-building thought rager, not the soft but firm, simple but clear intensity of Valerie. He just couldn't deal with it.

Now it was clear to him that, at the time, his still fragile ego was scared of her unassuming but strong Self. Her parents had been psychologists, and she had never learned the ways of the "real world" and thus needed his tutelage. When she instead began to simply love him in return, he had to end it. Damn, there was a theme here, he just had never seen it before; first Valerie, then Rachel. Maybe he had been surrounded by this all his life in one form or another, he just hadn't seen it for what it was, he couldn't have, he had been completely blind.

"Now you are no longer that. You see things differently and that is only possible because your eyes are opening. So what do you see?"

What did he see? Good question. And the only thing he could say was that he could see himself as that story and that he could see that who was seeing the story was really him as well, but felt unknown and yet deeply connected, like a person you meet who you swear you've known for lifetimes. There was a sense of timelessness with this feeling, as though he didn't exist. But he knew for the first time in his life that he was, in fact, real, but more real than he had ever been before, just not real in the old story sort of way. Surreal.

"'Ethereal' would be more precise. Welcome to the real world."

flying leap

* * *

Ether-real, that which was the ether was, in fact, real. He had studied this conception before. The ether had originated from Greek mythology, where one of the gods' names had been Aether, the god of the upper sky, where the gods breathed, far beyond the human realm, where the dense and heavy air was breathed. It morphed into the idea of anything without material substance, the way he was feeling now. Not material, but here somehow, *with* his body in a way, but not *in* it. How was this possible, and most of all, was this really happening or was he just making it all up? He looked at the bird, who looked back at him with an expression of "you are kidding, right?" written all over its beak. He had to laugh. That was the point, wasn't it? He was indeed making it all up, everything-in-its-entirety-all-of-the-time.

"I'm glad you're catching on."

"So why do we make up such a shit story?" he said, more to himself. "I mean, here we are, we only have one life,"—the bird looked up with granola in its beak and one expectant proverbial eyebrow raised—" ... as far as we can *remember* anyways, and then we create this." He stretched out his arms to include the whole planet. "*This* is the best we can come up with?"

Hell, he wasn't sure he wanted to be part of a world like that. Until the day before he had been one

94

of the best storymakers around and hadn't thought anything of it. But his story had come to an end, or rather, he had reached the point of ending it the only way he knew how because he did not want to be part of the world any longer. And now he had died, except not in the way he had expected, and he wanted to be part of that world even less now, only differently than the day before. What an effect a day could have.

Another memory of his previous life appeared. He was at an Avis rental center somewhere in Europe on one of his many trips talking to the lady behind the counter. He had realized they didn't give a shit about his President's Club level there, but he wanted that double upgrade—as a matter of fact, he wanted the Mercedes outside in the lot. He was doing one of his reads on this woman and knew exactly how to work her to get what he needed. So he leaned across the counter, put on his most charming grin, and did everything to make the woman feel good. He put her in a state of mind that was more relaxed so she would feel compelled to give him the upgrade. She would feel good, and he would feel good, and everybody would win.

Only they didn't and they hadn't. He was literally shaking in disgust at the feeling he was experiencing with this memory. The memory was so invasive,

95

so intimate and disrespectful at the same time, so violating, that he almost couldn't stand it. But at the time it had been normal, it had made sense. It had all been invisible to him and the woman, none of it had been real, because they'd been living out their own stories and happened to intersect. But they hadn't known that this was going on. They couldn't have. And yet it was going on all the time for everyone. Including him.

"And it was and is all quite innocent. Everyone is doing the best given what they know at any moment. Whatever makes sense in their story at the time is what they will succumb to. That is how you lived your entire life as well, and there is nothing *wrong* with that, but it is very *limited*. And it keeps people in a constant state of disconnectedness, which comes at a price. You just described that very well."

He was staring almost through the bird as he was reflecting on all this. It all seemed insurmountable and overwhelming to him. He had barely become aware of his own story and already wanted to give up.

"You are just beginning to wake up. This is all new and fresh for you, and you are still losing your mind here. This is but a beginning. As this new perspective takes hold, things can get a little confusing. Don't worry, this is normal."

He felt as though he needed to stretch his internals, not physically, but differently; make more room in here, out here, all here, to be able to see this new world. That's what it felt like.

"But why the hell don't we create a better world than the one we're in? I mean, most of the time we live in fear, whether it's other people not liking us, failure, not having enough in some way—hell, there are plenty of people right now on this earth who fear for their very life." He took a deep breath. "I was totally into that world, I owned it. I was right in the middle of it, playing the game. Except now that expression means something completely different. It *is* just a game in a way, isn't it?"

"You can see it that way, but of course it goes back to the observation that it's all *made up*. Everything. There is nothing and no thing that is not made up. Look at this with some reflection. It answers all your questions that you have about humanity, doesn't it? Whenever someone becomes aware of this fact, something changes in the world, in their world. Awareness is a powerful and tricky thing. Once you have it, it is impossible to lose. Awareness awards you not only the ability to become aware of what you have done thus far in your life in terms of how you made up your story, it also lets you become an active creator in your story; it allows you to craft the very world you live in."

"Wait a second, that doesn't quite fly for me. I still live in a world of circumstances, I have to deal with things around me, people and events, so it is being crafted without my participation. A lot of times I just have to deal with the fallout of other people's actions or simple acts of nature. How am I crafting *that*?"

The bird hopped up on the windowsill so it could catch some rays. "Well, I think you know the answer to this yourself. You have had many moments in your life story where you thought that someone or something was what you were dealing with, but that is only what it looked like from your limited perspective, the perspective as it pertained to you, and that is exactly where you are looking from right now." It closed its eyes and tilted its head towards the sun. "So why don't you give it another try."

Geez, this bird was never easy. Limited perspective, huh. So what if he took a grander perspective? Everything's made up. If everything was made up, then there must be someone making it up, right? Was there only one making it up, the big kahuna, or was everyone on earth making it up? What if he stretched his perspective a little further, like the universe? What then? Was the idea of the universe also made up? But by whom? His head started to hurt.

"That would be you bumping into the walls of

your limitations. Never feels quite right." The bird opened its eyes and turned to him. "Don't go too far in your musings when it doesn't make sense yet. Stick with what feels right, what gives you a deeper understanding and helps you see more. We will only ever understand that which we can understand."

"Okay, so let's go with this idea of how it's all made up, I like that. That feels good to me and makes sense at that gut level. It's wild to see my own life that way, to see it as something I have actually made up all along, something that I owned, but only because I became it. If everyone is doing this, and most of us are doing it unconsciously, everything we ever say and do makes sense to us, within the story. Once I see the story, what makes sense completely changes. And if I can see my story and see that I am the one making it up, then why would I choose to make up a story that terrorizes me? The suffering that comes with being the story and becoming a victim to circumstance is only real as long as the story is *me*. Once I am not the story, but the creator of the story, I can make up whatever I want—hot damn, that is pretty cool!"

"But what if your girlfriend leaves you and someone steals all your money? They are doing this to you, aren't they?"

"Well, in a way, yes, but also no, because all that

has happened here is that we intertwined our stories in total unawareness and everyone played the part that made sense to them. Everyone was crafting their own story, and my story included that I didn't really love my girlfriend and wanted her to leave, that I didn't heed my own gut feelings about my accountant. I chose to continue on in my story the way I did, and those people never had any power over that decision. None. I can see that so clearly now. I decided to make up my story the way I did. Period. They were never responsible for it." He was really enjoying this. "That does not mean that my story can't be about being a victim all my life, or being alone or a loser or a murderer or a drug addict, a power monger, an egomaniac, a good Samaritan , and on and on it goes. Holy shit, we do make it all up. And sometimes we change our story but remain the story nonetheless, and sometimes we *wake up* to the story and are no longer doomed to play it out unconsciously. That is true." That was such a freeing feeling.

"And the truth shall set you free," the bird said gently.

* * *

It was as though he had never heard that line before. It made sense. The truth was that everyone was making up a story, and thus all was made up—

moment to moment. This was not his or the bird's opinion, it wasn't about right or wrong; it was the truth.

"Well, I don't want to suggest there is only one Truth. It simply means that whenever you *see* beyond the limitations of your current state, it is an observation. When we can observe something, we don't have any judgment in the matter, affording us to see it in its virgin state if you will. That is its truth. The unimpeded observance of how it *is*, is truth."

He remembered another piece of his life story. He was fifteen years old and hanging out with friends who were drinking and smoking pot. He tried it as well, he didn't really want to, but he felt that he had to because everyone was doing it and he didn't want to be the loser of course. He didn't like the feeling of being high, he also didn't like the feeling of being tipsy, then drunk, then completely wasted. He also almost coughed up a lung and thought that the taste of alcohol was gross, but he kept going anyways. The next morning he woke up in his own puke, with no recollection of the night before, in a front yard he didn't recognize. Oh, and he was missing his pants. Now, at that moment he knew he was never going to do this again, not because of some moral judgment, but simply because he hadn't enjoyed any aspect of the experience. He got himself home, thankfully his parents were still asleep, and went to bed. Within the next few days he was able to laugh along with everyone about that crazy night and all the shit they had pulled, but his heart wasn't in it, and when his buddies decided to do it again, he told them he didn't care one way or the other what they did, but that he would be sitting out. At first they made fun of him, but he could see that they had their own doubts and insecurities about it all, and he simply let them be and didn't feel like he had to say anything or defend it. He just saw it so clearly for himself, without any expectations of them or himself. It was his truth, plain and simple. And because he didn't react to their bullshit, he could hang with them anyways, the eternal designated driver. He had never done a drug or drank alcohol after that.

"As I mentioned yesterday, this always has been one of the authentic parts about you. It was your truth, but more importantly, it was *a* truth. You could see the process and the stories being played out around the drinking and getting high and it simply didn't belong to you. That is the beauty of seeing stories clearly in others or yourself; it brings clarity to you and the situation."

"That makes sense, but how is it possible that we get to have moments in our lives when we can see these stories so clearly, yet we just go on living right back in them as if nothing happened?"

"Well, it's safe, familiar, easy—and most of all, habit. Don't forget, at that point you still *are* the story, which means that even though you may have seen things from a different perspective, the underlying foundation of you-being-the-story is fully intact. Your sense of self and who you are is completely rooted in this charade and will even fight to the death to maintain its 'identity' as you have found out yourself."

He saw once more what a grip his ego or story had had on his life and shuddered.

"What happens in those moments is what's commonly referred to as insight, a gut feeling, a hunch. It describes what happens when you step out of your story and have access to the real You, giving you a clear vision of what is actually going on—that you are *not* the story. With that perspective comes immediate clarity about what is happening. No guess work. That's what real certainty is." The bird stretched its wings. "And then most people write it off to chance or luck that they had this insight. They don't know what it actually is. At worst they don't even pay attention to it and at best they hope for more moments like that and turn it into something."

That he understood, he had done so countless times. He had learned to look for his inner voice, but he never had been able to figure out how to make it happen more often. He'd tried to recreate situations in which he had had insights; he came up with all kinds of habits and rules around them; at one point he was even convinced that spending his evening making a particular dish, while having *The Godfather* on in the background, and afterwards taking a bath with essential oils and candles (and no, he had never told anyone this of course) would produce insight. So basically within his life story he had made up a chapter called "How to Create Insight," hoping that would work. But it hardly ever did.

"How could it? It is not the circumstance that gives you insight, it is the very fact that you are able to *step outside* of the circumstance that awards you a bigger perspective. Insight lets you see the inner workings of the story, it shows you that it's there in the first place. From that vantage point, everything else is just details."

"'I want to know God's thoughts; the rest are details,'" he said. "I have always loved that line but never thought of it the way I do now." Funny how all along there had been so many signposts right there in front of him lighting the way through the dark places in his life. All he really had to do was pay attention and follow the crumbs.

* * *

That brought something else to his mind. He had spent all that time studying the spiritual tomes and had gone to what he considered great lengths to be a good student; in the end he even believed he had somewhat of a clue. But one thing had always been hard for him to wrap his mind around: the idea that there was nothing to accomplish in order to be en-enlightened about his place in the universe. He figured he would at least try to be a good person, a searcher of truth, a catalyst for change and positivity in the world, someone who would want to add something good to the world and as a result end up a better person with insight into the mysteries of it all. But he had also read that all beings were already accom-plished, and that there was nothing to do or achieve in order to be fully realized. He had never been able to reconcile those two ideas in his mind. Now he felt the presence of another possibility.

"That is one interesting dichotomy," the bird ob-served, rubbing its nonexistent chin. "So what pos-sibility is entering your mind?"

"Well, I'm thinking that if we simply create sto-ries, in those stories we also make up all these ideas about who we are, what we like and don't like, what works and what doesn't, what's right and what's wrong, and those change all the time; I mean, as far as humans go, we have had all kinds of fucked-up ideas about ourselves throughout history. But I'm getting stuck here again ... because in making everything up, we also make up the idea of everything coming in twos, right?" He sat back in his chair and crossed his arms.

The bird looked at him quizzically. "Is that a real question or a rhetorical one?"

"I guess a real question; I wasn't sure when I asked."

"Remember when we talked about the idea of the story as another way to describe the ego?" He nodded. "Well, that answers your question, doesn't it? Reflect on this for a moment."

They both sat in silence for what seemed an eternity, but he found his mind in a milder form of overdrive than the day before, and he couldn't quite grab hold of anything solid. "Help me out, please."

The bird implied a sigh. "Creating this separate, disconnected entity only works if you put yourself apart from or in opposition to some-thing or someone. Only in doing so can you experience yourself as separate. That is duality. That doesn't mean it's *truth*, but it does make it real to you. Within that duality you create all opposing ideas. Thus you also create the idea of incompleteness, and within that system you are never accomplished enough, good enough, nice enough ... or evil enough, if that's your story. You can't be, because of duality." The bird flew into the living room and sat on a pillow. He followed.

"But how does that connect to my question about not trying harder to be a better person? I don't quite get that yet."

"It is only within the idea of duality that incompleteness can exist, because it stands in opposition to completeness. Thus it is with accomplishment— you can never reach the idea of being accomplished so long as you see the possibility of being unaccomplished."

The bird was definitely tickling his mind.

"Good. Tickling is good. Now, remember how I also said that none of what we are doing here is about you becoming a better person?"

"Kinda."

"What I meant was that you can try all your life to be a better person, and there is nothing wrong with that, but it only exists within the realm of your duality. Do you see that? Only when you can be a bad person, can you also be a better person."

That made sense.

"Seeing what you are beginning to see, the deeper reality of your story and knowing that you are creating it, as is everyone else, gives you the awareness to see that duality is simply part of the story, and with that understanding comes the ability to see it for what it is."

"That it's not *real* but only something that we make up ... and so I am free from having to define myself in that way. Neither one is really true, it's just a function of the story. That is wild. Because if I see the world that way, then I can see how it all plays itself out in the way people make it up, but that's it, nothing else."

The bird nodded. "And when you look at the world with that awareness, you can see that there is nothing you have to do or be to be perfect or better or anything like that, because you are no longer in opposition to anything. You are in observance of *what is* and get to freely create your participation in it."

There was this strange feeling rising up in him. A vastness filled with a very deep sense of knowing and calm. He closed his eyes. After a couple of minutes a new feeling began to form in his mind, he couldn't quite verbalize it yet, but it reminded him of the expression of the proverbial "brave new world." On the one hand he had learned all this new information, but at the same time he also *felt* different, and that's not how new information had impacted him in the past. He used to learn something new and then immediately find words and thoughts to describe it intelligently; most of all he would integrate it into his existent story. If it changed his story, then he would make sure that he was in control of this change, and if it was impossible to control the new information by integrating it somehow, he would simply reject it as silly or wrong, or just not for him. Funny how he had always made sure that his world made sense. That's what everybody was doing, wasn't it? He opened his eyes.

"Now I get what you meant when you said that everyone is doing the best they can, given what they know at any moment. I have always struggled with that idea, because it meant to me that someone like Hitler or Stalin was a good person after all, that they were doing their best. But what it actually means is that what they did was all they could do given what they knew, given what their story presented them as options. It's not about a moral measuring stick of good, better, best—it's about their unconscious participation in their story that very much dictated their logic and reality and limited their choices to what they were. Right?"

The bird was sitting on the coffee table now and nodded. "Yes, that's a nice description, and given your experience with your own life story, you can understand how compelling it is. It is absolutely real to you when you are in the middle of it. For some people their story includes what you might judge to be suffering or torture, but also happiness and joy. However, all of those still exist in the realm of opposites. Whenever you are living in your story, your thinking will automatically produce more chapters for the story to continue; your ego will make sure of its own existence as a default. Everyone chooses every aspect of their story, every step of the way."

That didn't sit well with him. "Wait a second. Are you trying to tell me that some baby who is beaten to death by its drunken parent is *choosing* that? Or that a woman who gets raped and killed is *choosing* that as part of her story? What about the countless innocent victims in wars throughout history? How could they all have chosen that?" He was definitely having trouble with this idea.

"I am not *trying* to tell you anything. I am simply describing the process to you. It is your choice to observe it yourself. And as to your question, you have to remember that this is a description of how things are in an unaware and unconscious world. Look at the state of your world. You have said yourself that it's not pretty. This is a direct result of the shallow level of awareness people on earth generally have. But for a few exceptions, the people of this planet operate in a very asleep manner, and this has consequences, the results of which you can watch on your evening news every night."

"But how does that play into my question?"

The bird shook its head. "You are not listening very well, are you? Look. The vast majority of people are not consciously creating their life story. Life is happening *to them*, at least most of the time, and this puts in place an incredible limitation on the choices available. It places you in dependence of everyone else's story, and you feel that others have power over you. This is why the drunk parent is a 'victim' to his own deluded mind, the baby has not learned to create its story; all the murderers and their victims are living their stories out with each other, because that's all they know. All of this is quite innocent and simply is as it is, but it is still their choice."

He was struggling with this, but at the same time there was a new view of things coming into his mind, a view where he felt that this somehow made sense. It was still very hard for him to consider that experience as a whole was a result of choice. But his largest hurdle was that choice implied freedom, and if you were free to choose, why choose such a horrible experience?

"Because that is the only choice available to you if you are not awake or aware enough to see your creative power in choosing your life story moment to moment. In this way life happens *to* you, it is not lived *by* you. Once you see that, not only do your choices change, you have many more available to you."

He was listening with a deeper ear now.

"Don't you see? People aren't consciously choosing to commit atrocities against each other; quite on the contrary, they are deeply unconscious. Only someone completely unaware of the truth that they choose everything in their life could end up creating such a hell for themselves and others. They may even tell you that they are consciously and freely choosing what they are doing, but this is a statement from the very limited vantage point of which they are choosing; a place made up entirely by them, filled with opposites, hardships, and effort. From within that life story, 'consciousness' is at best a nice dream and at worst a nightmare."

Another memory came into view. In grad school, he had done an internship at a psychiatric outpatient clinic working with "delinquent youths," as they were now labeled, who had committed some hefty crimes; after all, the courts had ordered them into therapy. Some had hurt people badly, some had parents who had kicked them out, most had done drugs, and all were in pretty rough shape. But he saw an innocence in those kids; they didn't scare him because he saw how wounded they were, how lost and lonely. He talked to the part of them that seemed untouched by their bad experiences, by their own ideas about how

tough they were and had to be. He simply looked beyond it and related to that in them which was whole.
There was nothing missing, they just couldn't see
past the stories people had ingrained in them from
early on, stories they believed and made their own.
He talked to that deeper part in them as if it were
in plain view, and most of those kids came around.
They would argue, then believe, and then finally see
it as well. He knew every time when it happened,
something would light up in them and they would
literally change right in front of his eyes, and they
would never be the same again after that. Now he
could see they had simply bought into the worst
story someone had made up about them. Some went
back to their story, some completely changed it and
others stepped outside of it and began to craft it consciously and actively. But all were changed by *seeing*
themselves the way he did. They didn't have to accomplish anything to be "fixed" or "good."

"They were already accomplished, weren't they?"
the bird asked. And he nodded.

Absolutely. He had never seen it that way before,
but now it made sense and it felt really good. So if
they were accomplished, they had been that way
even in the thick of their drama, in the middle of the
chaos that was their life—that was the only way he
had been able to see it. If it was true for those kids,

how could it not be true for anyone else? But could every single human on earth be a fully accomplished being beyond the limitations of their own stories?

The bird didn't even have to react.

"That makes sense to me, I admit, and I can even see it in my own life story. I mean, I can see myself like I used to see those kids; underneath all that massive pile of bullshit called 'me' is the same untouchable wholeness." But something still didn't quite fit. "Even though that really hits home for me now, I still have trouble understanding or maybe even believing that a person would choose to be beaten or raped or killed." He looked to the bird for an explanation, he was willing to understand it even though he didn't know how or what exactly.

The bird looked as if it were pondering its answer quite carefully. "I am not sure if you are ready or even *can* understand what I am about to tell you." He sat up straight in preparation for another mind-bending exercise.

"The short answer is yes, every being in form chooses every single aspect of their experience in form, no matter how unlikely that may appear. That is the truth."

He was about to protest, but the bird held up one wing to stop him.

"Let me explain, as this is very important for your

further inquiries into the nature of things. I am now asking you to join me in looking at your world and all the humans in it from a larger perspective. Are you willing to do that?"

"I think so," he said, with slight trepidation.

"Every being in form on this planet is an aspect of a larger field. It is not a physical field, of course, but a field of limitless energy that takes on similarly limitless forms of limitless kinds. This is not something you can conceptualize—your human form is simply not designed for this. But you also know that it is there, you feel it, you sometimes suspect that it is there, you make yourself believe that it's there and you give it numerous names and concepts. Before you enter into this specific human form from and through that field, you know exactly what you're signing up for, the whole deal, the story, your part in the story, your awareness of the story. So when you come into this world, you fulfill your story as you see fit. If you are a baby who gets murdered by a drunken parent, then you *freely choose* to be that baby and to go through this particular experience. So does the drunken parent. I know this is hard to hear from your vantage point, still being so close to considering your own story as real, but that's how it works. Never forget that you can choose at all times to create a different story, or to become aware of the story so you may more freely choose your participation in this human experience. That way you can be *in* the world without being *of* it."

He realized that even though the explanation the bird had given him was at the very least stretching his world some more and maybe even seemed somewhat incredulous, it made him feel good. The idea that every human being could choose their life in every aspect, and that we even made choices about our lives ahead of time, was reassuring. "Ahead of time," was hitting him as well, as though choices were made all the time, outside of time, ahead of a life experience within time. He couldn't completely understand what he was contemplating, but these thoughts were coming to him on their own and they felt right. The world made more sense this way. He had lost a friend a couple of years back who had been kidnapped on a trip through the backwaters of Mongolia; he was ultimately tortured to death. He had been very upset by this and had even used his financial resources in an attempt to find the perpetrators. He had never found peace with this situation and kept having nightmares for a while about his friend suffering. But now he was daring to entertain the possibility that his friend had chosen this exit strategy from his life long before he had gotten here and thus had been a co-creator in this event. It still seemed crazy, but it resonated reassuringly deep within him.

"Remember that we are speaking from a perspective beyond the human experience," the bird said. "It is important to keep that in mind. There is only so much that can be explained in human terms, and from the human position only so much can be understood fully. But what you feel is the field talking to you. It is letting you know through this experiential moment that you are constantly in-formation, you are part of the information of the field in-formation in an individuated form—at all times."

"Huh, that's a different way to look at yourself, I guess ... always in formation. So everything is a work in progress then, never quite done, but also part of this field you talk about, so by that view everything *is* done and perfect, because I would assume this field contains ... well ... I don't even know how to think about this, frankly ... but I guess it is sort of like all the information is available, and I am thinking totality here, but I can't think it really, either ... " He shook his head and stood up.

"You are running into the built-in limitations that are part of the human form. It's a measure of protection, if you will."

That fit with the experience of his tickled mind, the way he used to stretch it and then feel as though he were bumping into that limitation of sorts, that border or veil, so close he could maybe pass through, but ultimately impenetrable. In those moments there had increasingly been an echo of a certainty that there was something beyond all this—this "thing" called life—that was in charge somehow, but also was waiting for him to find it, to see it, and he had always figured that this would happen at death, the big revelation, the epiphany that would not only put everything in perspective but also cradle you in that moment of passing over. The One.

At this, the bird snickered. "Are you still holding on to that idea of 'The Truth' out there, waiting for you?"

"So there isn't one central truth?"

"Sure there is, but it doesn't matter in the least, because if you were to talk about it, you would simply be making it up. Right?"

The bird always managed to pull a fast one on him. His idea of Truth, the one that explained it all, the one behind it all, the one that all sprang from, had always been comforting.

"Well, in that story of yours, you needed a lot of comforting."

"Shit, that's true, isn't it? Such a big part of my story was about being spiritual. I mean, I was good at the spiritual game, anyone who met me would have thought I was all about it. But the way I see it now, apart from being a bullshit story, is that I felt so insignificant ... part of something, but still so alone ... having that idea of this grand Truth waiting for me, ready to take me in, was comforting. And it gave me a sense of importance—because I thought I knew about it."

"That is true, my friend. And it doesn't make any difference how you choose to think about Truth or God or Allah or the Supreme Intelligence or the Universe or the Big Nothing or whatever you may call it. How you choose does not matter in the least." The bird hopped on his knee. "*That* you choose is the important piece."

"You mentioned that before, the choice thing. Why is it so important?"

"Because without choice there would be no story. No-thing to make up. And if there were no stories to make up, you couldn't choose to be your story, now could you? And if you couldn't choose to be your story and thus choose to be unconscious, then you could never choose to wake up from it, either. There would not be any experience, and by that I do mean any experience, human and beyond."

That was an interesting thought. Choice made it all possible. Without choice, there would be nothing. Or no-thing. He smiled.

flying leap

"So if my parents hadn't made the choices they made within their stories—which they chose—I wouldn't have been born to begin to choose my story and to make all the choices that I made, which sometimes other people chose to be impacted by—or have an impact on, which made them choose whatever they did and so on and so forth." His mind was facing one of those cognitive dissonances. If everything, no, every thing, was in existence because of choice, then when and where or how did it start? Had there ever been an original choice made? The choice that there will be choice? Or had choice always existed? But how could something always exist? And if there had been an original choice, who or what made it and why?

"That, my friend, is the question of all questions, and what you are looking at here cannot be *seen* in your current form, but it can be *described* and *felt*. The original choice was the Big Bang, it was the field or God realizing itself, it was the Supreme Intelligence wanting to experience itself, it was the cosmos saying hello and moving from Being to Doing."

* * *

He sat there on the couch and couldn't hold a thought, nothing seemed to fit right then, nothing was *interesting* enough to think about. What an odd feeling. His mind wasn't blank, it wasn't struggling for an answer or concept, it was simply there. Not empty, not full, just there. He had no words or thoughts or ideas.

"That is the *experience* of your Self looking at you."

Really? That was it? Somehow he had expected it to be a bigger deal. Instead he just sat and ... well, no and.

"The experience of Being is not about doing. You can't *do* being, you can only be it. This is nothing exciting, it is also not the opposite of boring; it simply *is*. The closest you can come to Being in human beingness is to experience the absence of the duality of thought—which is where you find yourself right now. Being is not in the duality, and thus it is not part of that or subject to that, which puts it outside of the realm of positive or negative, happy or sad, exhilarating or depressing, and so on." The bird took a deep breath. "There is a common belief out there among people who are what you call 'spiritual seekers' that the attainment of a state of being is something that comes with a lot of hoopla, or that you have to suffer to 'reach' it, or live a specific kind of life by specific rules. None of that is necessary." It looked at him again. "Because you are already accomplished, remember?"

That blew his mind some more. Basically he had

spent all these years in his own spiritual story, waiting for this very moment to come, to happen to him,
and yes, he had expected it to be some kind of big
deal, but now he just turned to the feeling again, and
there it was, an incredible silence, a reassuring silence that felt alert and alive at the same time. Who
knew?

"Well, as a matter of fact, no one knows anything—
ever. In this human form, that is an impossibility."

He raised his eyebrow. "Well, I know my name, I
know what I ate for breakfast just now, I know that
I wanted to kill myself yesterday—"

The bird interrupted him with a laugh and hopped
onto the couch. "Unbelievable," it mumbled.

"What?!"

"Really? You have to ask? I mean, really?"

What was he missing here?

"Apparently a lot more than I thought."

"Alright already, enlighten me! What do you want
from me?"

"To reflect instead of coming up with the first au-
tomated response based on your lifetime of storytell-
ing, a story so full of 'facts' and 'knowing' that it led
you to the most unknown of all moments you could
possibly bring yourself to, your death … "

But what did that have to do with the knowing
thing?

"Everything!"

For a moment he didn't know what to make of this. "So you're telling me that I don't know those things? Is that it?"

"Well, from the limited and time-bound perspective of your small ego story self, you indeed seemingly know all this; but from the perspective of your Self that you just experienced a moment ago, not so much."

How did this fit? He sat back and decided to be open to an answer. He looked around the room and noticed how beautifully the sun rays were streaming in through the windows and how he could see some dust particles dancing in the light. Then he heard the birds chirping in the big old maple outside the window and he looked at the room in its entirety and it was what it was. It didn't mean anything in particular, it was there, and it was vibrant. And a thought drifted into his mind that said to him that what he had been talking about was the *idea* of knowing. And on top of that, the things he had described to himself had been made up in the first place, and before they had been made up they didn't exist and there was no way of knowing whether they ever would, and once they had been, they immediately turned into part of his story, a memory, and this memory always changed, depended on his mood, on what was going on at the moment he was having the memory—so in essence, he never really knew his memory either, it was all fluid, always in motion. The only thing he felt was that he was here now.

The bird nodded. "Was that so hard?"

With this he decided he needed some fresh air. "You wanna come?" he asked the bird.

"Sure, I'll meet you downstairs."

He passed the doorman and got out into the street, looked around and was amazed at all the activity going on around him. So many people. As he started down the block he noticed again that everything seemed more vibrant; at this he really had to laugh, because he had always thought of it as stupid when, in so many of the books he had read, the authors would say this ... and yet it was happening to him. He sat himself in the grass across the street in the small park and simply took it all in. As he looked at the old oak tree right above him he was stunned. There was a silent aliveness in that tree, in the leaves; it was so quiet and yet alive. He started laughing again at the seeming absurdity of this, was he turning into some weird freak here?

Then he realized that he didn't know where the bird had gone. He saw a bunch of pigeons being fed by an old lady, but he was sure his wasn't among them and started to worry. What if it had gone without saying goodbye? He wasn't ready for it to go; there was so much more to ask, he didn't have enough practice yet to make it all stick—

"Isn't it amazing how quickly your old story can sneak in?" The bird landed next to him in the grass and sat down.

"It was fear again, I know it. It's so gross compared to the way I was feeling right before."

"And you did that without me on your mind."

That was true. "What is this strange sensation I am having looking at the tree?" He lay down and lost himself in the leaves.

"This is what happens when you're actually *present*. Being present lets you see what is; you don't see the *idea* of whatever you are looking at, you don't just get to have your thoughts and experience them, you see without the label, the automatic story version. It's as though you are tuned into a different frequency. You can have the experience of the other form in a more pure, undefined, and unlimited manner. Just think about how you used to walk around the world as a little child. Everything was new at all times, and as you asked people about the things you saw, they gave you labels and definitions and you began to form a story around the form, and thus the form turned into the story. It's what you call education."

flying leap

"You're right. As a kid I couldn't wait to fall asleep really fast, so I could wake up as soon as possible and have a new day with new adventures and new stuff to discover." He began to feel all warm inside thinking about his childhood that way. "So basically we are born and have no clue that we are a separate being, and then we start to develop this idea of being a 'me' and all the people around us are modeling this and teaching us this and by doing so they are simply teaching us how to start our own story and voilà, we fall asleep."

And then people passed on their stories to their kids and each other, only reconfirming them and keeping them real, and it went on forever, until someone would wake up and see it and choose to stop it. Thinking about this, the insanity of the world made total sense to him. Everybody was running around doing the best they could, passing along their stories and arguing about whose story was more real, more important or more right, and thus recreating the same basic stories over and over again. Kinda depressing.

"You are seeing the process at work here; the depression comes from turning your awareness into a self-absorbed idea about how things should not be that way. This will simply pull you back into another story about the state of things. The one about how you have seen the truth and have to tell everyone about it or try to change the world for the better."

"And bingo, I am back to judging and that duality shit. I get it."

The bird seemed quietly content.

fli

ght

He lay in the grass for a while, enjoying his new state. So much had been new in the past couple of days, new was becoming the new old, and at that he had to laugh. What a completely different experience he was having now. It would have been unimaginable for him only thirty-six hours ago. How could he have spent all these years missing what was right inside of him, around him, everywhere the whole time? How lucky he had been to meet the bird.

Wait a second though. Had it really been luck? Had he not *chosen* to meet the bird? Had he not *chosen* to listen to it and begin this conversation in the first place? This little change in his view of events completely changed his view of his situation—no, his whole life ... shit, his death and everything else—again.

Then he noticed how unaware he had become of his surroundings during his musings. This was very tricky business, this presence thing. Once he noticed,

the tree's vibrancy charged back into his consciousness and he immediately got lost in it, the movement
of the branches and the leaves, the wind blowing,
and he found himself having fun shifting the focus
of conscious awareness from one thing to another.
He closed his eyes again and noticed that another
underlying quality was coming through, underneath
the sounds and sights, the smells and sensations,
was a whole other ... he couldn't describe it ... not
a sensation, not a five senses sort of thing ... not a
thought either. It was as though there was something very silent and alive and *big* underneath all
the activity—and he could feel it. He felt something
close to goose bumps going up his body, then up the
back of his neck, over the top of his head, over his
eyes ... then his heart suddenly beat faster and the
whole sensation settled over his senses like a warm
blanket. He focused on his breathing and wondered
whether he was having a heart attack, but he knew
he wasn't. As he kept breathing, his heart calmed
down. And even though his eyes were still closed, he
could feel that everything looked different, how odd,
so he opened his eyes and realized that everything
was different. He couldn't make sense of it; he knew
what he was looking at, and yet it was not the same
as it had been just moments before.

"That is the experience of the field in-formation,

unimpeded by the thoughts you may have formed over the years—all the thoughts you have made up and that made you, the ideas of what everything is, how everything is and what it means. When you experience the world from within your Self and thus outside the story, you are witness to the field forming and thus realize your place within it." The bird looked at him. "The physical sensation you were experiencing with this is normal; however, it is also quite new for you and at first may be a bit disconcerting, even though it is normal. What you were picking up as the underlying quality is the field I talked about before. The feeling is you being aware of it."

He didn't know what to say, and didn't want to say anything anyway. It would have distracted him from what was going on.

"I am glad you are feeling this," the bird said in a very quiet and calm voice that resonated within him the same way the field had. "This is what is going on all the time, you are looking behind the curtain. Remember how you jumped on this when we met? How you said that you had suspected all your life there was 'something else going on?' Well, here it is."

"Holy shit, I know what you are saying, I really do. This feels so much more like home than anything else I've felt before." He was looking around and everything was ... well, it simply was. All the people, the smells, the grass, the trees, all of it, it just was there, but man, it was so there. But it wasn't a big deal or anything, it didn't even feel particularly positive or negative, it was just *there*. But there was so much there that he wanted to swim in it.

"You actually *are* swimming in it, all the time," the bird said. "It is impossible to *not* be in it, because you *are* it. Not even just a part of it, but it. There is no separation between the you you may think you are and the field. You are the field and the field is you. It's all there all at once, being *expressed* in all these different ways." He looked at the bird and was overwhelmed, or rather felt even more immersed in the feeling he was having. This is what he had pretended to himself all these years in his old life, this state he found himself in right now had been what he had wanted to achieve, get to, reach somehow, like some pie in the sky, the pearl you get as a reward for working hard enough on yourself, studying the way of the enlightened hard enough and long enough. And here he was, and it *was* all encompassing, but it wasn't a big deal at all.

"So if everyone is in the same boat as I am, then everyone is also creating everything all the time, and everyone is this field as well. So it's almost as though we are condensed or localized energy bundles through which this form called a human life is experienced. Right?" He looked at the bird.

"I honestly could not have said it any better. That is a very accurate description."

He felt an even deeper kinship with the bird.

"Once you are the actual experience of something, it also becomes completely obvious and clear. It is as though you have been shown a magic trick and get to see how it works, only now you can perform it, change it, evolve it, and really enjoy the creativity in creating magic, and then be part of the experience with an audience that is mystified with the magic. It really is lovely."

He liked that very much. He had always enjoyed magic and was reminded of when he used to play with it. The biggest challenge for him had been to know how a trick worked, and to perform it for others, all the while thinking that the trick was so obvious, so easy, that everyone would figure it out immediately. Except people wouldn't. He realized that what made magic work was that the mechanics of the trick were hidden, and that as long as you made sure of that and told a nice story while performing, the trick would continue to work. Even though everyone *knew* that it was a trick, the audience wanted to believe it, and that was exactly how all human life experience was, except that the trick was what everyone believed to be *life*, completely buying into the tricks that their own thoughts were playing on them, knowing deep down it was all just a trick, but not wanting to find out how it worked, because it would change everything. Having become the story it was easier to continue in that way than to risk waking up from it and finding out that there was no one to blame, no one was wrong(ed), because everyone was making it up all along. Life would not be the same if everyone realized this, if everyone saw that they were nothing but a localized, individuated conductor of energy, producing form. That they weren't a big deal or an insignificant deal, but that they were the all of everything, expressed in form.

"All this feels great, but I don't see how me having this experience actually changes anything. I mean, I spent most of my adult life studying this stuff, surrounded mostly by like-minded people, but yet it was never *real*, it never affected me in this deep way. I was still stuck in this story of mine, it was just a story with a spiritual spin." He could feel a heaviness creeping up inside him.

"You are correct, and what you are describing may have been what you had created, and it made sense to you at the time, as everything does to everyone at all times, but that is not the point of what you are doing here right now." The bird hopped on his chest and looked at him intensely. "You are feeling the reality of it all, limited in scope as it may be in your human form, but you feel it nonetheless. Thus your life has changed forever. Don't kid yourself, there is no going back for you now. That sense of heaviness you are feeling is simply your awareness of the story creeping back inside your consciousness, whispering in your ear 'come over here, I am the real deal, become me, become the story, where everything makes sense in that familiar way.' But your awareness lets you see the heaviness which indicates this story is working at a lower frequency if you will, that it is in fact heavier than where you are right now." The bird did a 180 on his chest with spread wings. "Look around and look within and then I ask you to decide which one *feels* better."

Well, that was easy enough. This feeling of the field was definitely the way to go. No question.

"Good. That is what you know, that is who you are, and that is all that matters. The rest are details." The bird winked at him.

But even if he got to live his life in this feeling, even just a big part of the time, what good would it do beyond him? How would it change anything, when the world looked as though it needed so much changing?

"Why don't you let the world worry about that, my friend. Your world is changed, your world is the one you create, your world is the one you live in, and you are now living in a very different world from even a moment ago. All has changed for you, the whole world has changed for you, and it will continue to do so. The point is that you cannot change anything but *your* world. It is not about anyone else, or the world 'out there,' it is about participating actively and creatively in *expression*, in whatever way you choose. However, now you get to do it with the added awareness of the process at work. And this has a very powerful effect."

It occurred to him that there really was no world "out there" anyways, he and everyone else on the planet were only living in their own individualized version of the world.

* * *

"You had mentioned 'need' yesterday and that we were going to talk about that later … "

"Yes." Silence.

"Well, what about it?"

The bird just looked at him. And then he realized that in all his conversations with people, all his discussions and arguments, he had always been so full of assumptions and expectations. Even his questions hadn't been really questions most of the time—they had been demonstrations of what he already knew,

138

while expecting the other person to give him what he wanted: more information to add to his reservoir. No unbridled curiosity anymore. Everything had been wrapped up in himself in some way, somehow. So when he had asked about need just then, he hadn't actually asked a question ...

"Let me try that again. I remember that yesterday you said something about need, and that we were going to talk about it later. Well, I am curious about that and am asking you whether you might have something to say about that right now." This felt a lot better.

"This is as good a time as any, I suppose. What would you like to know?"

Well, what did he want to know? He found that his brain wasn't working the same way anymore, he wasn't jumping to thoughts and answers as quickly as he used to, everything was a bit slower.

"Don't worry, that will get better, you are simply using your brain in a more natural way than you have in a very long time. It's like getting on a bike after twenty-five years without one; it takes a little while before you can ride without hands again."

"I am wondering about the function or purpose of need. I am not sure how it fits any longer to tell you the truth." He blinked and looked up in the sky, immediately feeling that wonderful mind tickle. "I used

139

to have needs a lot, maybe even more than anything else; having needs and being able to express them well meant that I was a self-assured person, someone who existed and needed to be taken seriously." It was so interesting to be able to look at his own ideas from the past this way; in a way, they seemed silly.

"Need is one of the biggest ego expressions there is," said the bird. "It is born out of the demands that the ego makes up in order to solidify its place in the world. It's part and parcel with keeping the story of you real; it is another way of attempting to create a sense of permanence if you will. For when you voice your needs, you are making yourself heard, you are demanding something from others, from the world—and often even from yourself—that shows that you are real. You will even say 'I have *real* needs.'"

He and the bird laughed and he could feel they were laughing for the same reason.

"If you look at it this way," the bird continued, "it is very obvious that need is a purely ego- or story-based idea and emotion. In need, there is no experience except the demands of your ego. That is it. There is no room for anything else. It is about you, about the expression and fulfillment of your demands, about making yourself more real to you and others. And then most everyone else you meet has needs as well, whether they express them or not, and thus you are

140

concerned with your needs all the time."

"So you're saying that need is bad? But would people still create anything if they didn't have needs? Doesn't the need to exist drive us to come up with stuff?" As those questions had finished forming in his mind, he already knew that they were old questions, and that the new questions and answers had not quite made it into his conscious mind yet.

"Well, it's a good thing then that we get to hang out," the bird said, popping back into his mind. "The story humans have created around need is the trickiest right after fear; it is completely ingrained in your idea of self. Need seems to be such a good thing on the surface. 'People need shelter and food,' you say, or 'All you need is love.' You speak of basic needs that have to be met for everyone. You connect it to the basic human dignity and that is your starting point. Need has made its entrance into the world as a basic and justified human emotion. And then you build from there. Who would dare question the need for food and shelter? But if you cannot question that, then you cannot question the basic concept of need."

"Wait a second. I don't think that the need for shelter and food is too much to ask for—they are *basic needs*, aren't they? I mean, we would die without food. Or am I missing something here?" This was weird, how he was feeling argumentative in his questions; something was off in him, he couldn't tell what, but it definitely didn't feel right. He was demanding an answer, a resolution from the bird.

"That's demand for you. It feels exactly the way you are feeling it right now. There is a certain pressure and indignation that comes with demands, much like need." The bird flapped its wings briefly and a few feathers drifted off. "I am about to tell you something that flies right in the face of your collective idea of self, so bear with me alright?" He nodded. "You don't *need* anything. You don't even *need* food. Let me be more specific. Your body does not *need* food. Your body simply carries out the functions it is designed to carry out to the best of its ability, given the circumstances it finds itself in. Period. The cells in your body do not know need, they simply function. Much like a flower doesn't *need* water—it grows when it gets enough of it, and it ceases to grow when it doesn't. When your body does not receive any food, it will simply continue to function as long as it can without it, and then it quits. It is not sad about this, it has no feeling about this, it simply is. You are the one who creates the need. You say that without food you will not be able to live. But who is saying that?"

"My ego, my story," he mumbled to himself. "That is true—we create the story that is attached to this body, this form, and call it 'me.' We become that story or me and since it is contained in that body of ours it makes total sense that we will do whatever we can to ensure its survival. And for that I *need* to give it food." Huh, that was very interesting. This implied it was a choice.

"Correctamundo," the bird said. "Everything is a choice. You choose to eat. You choose to be your story. You choose to live, to die, to need, to be happy, to be depressed—in other words, you choose whether to *do* or to *be*. When you choose to be, need falls away, because you are no longer the story. In order for you to be your story, need is required. Need is based in ego. Yes, it will make you create, and as always, there is nothing wrong with this—it is simply a hard way to live and to experience human form."

"But if we don't have any needs, what would drive me to do anything?"

"Have you ever seen a child who was not curious or creative? It is built in to the human experience that you should create through expression by exercising choice. Without need it just shows up in you differently, it has a different quality altogether, it shows up as inspiration, intuition, insight, curiosity, or even a revelation. The common denominator here is that you feel it without any particular outcome attached to it. It simply feels right. Need always has an outcome attached to it, a demand for fulfillment."

That was true. His needs had always been attached to him. Hell, even when he would say to someone that they needed to do something, see something, it was because *he* wanted them to. With need there was no experience except demands. He laughed at that. No Experience Except Demands = NEED.

"If I look back at my relationships, I can see how they were so focused on needs. 'I need you to say this or that, I need you to do this or that, you need to do this for me, you need to quit this or start that, I need to feel loved by you,' and on and on." That was very different from the loving feeling he had always imagined he would have with his future partner. He had messed that up royally. "Where does greed fit into this?"

"Greed is simply need on speed," said the bird matter-of-factly.

He lost it at that, laughing so hard it hurt. With that one sentence the bird had explained it completely. And for the first time he could see the humor in the life he had led. How innocently he had done the best he could, given what he had known at any time. It tickled him to no end. And he was crying tears of laughter this time.

After he calmed down, he looked at the bird and felt as though he wanted to give it a hug. What a funky little creature and a wild ride this had been thus far. "I totally get that now, the need thing. And what you said about greed ... " he laughed again, " ... makes total sense. As a matter of fact, I see the two of them intimately linked. So whether I need anything or greed anything, it is simply a matter of degree. Both never end, both are about me, and both perpetuate the idea of me as the story. Because if I can tell the world about my needs, or solidify them through greed, I make *me* more real. And then I even go and tell others that they can have needs, too—but only if mine are met as well. What a way to meet each other."

"As a matter of fact, you don't meet each other as much as you simply meet another expression of a story. It is by design a very disconnected way to be with another person. However, when you are no longer your story, need simply disappears and is replaced with preferences. You may prefer this food or activity or that one for the time being and that changes according to your choice. For when you are Being, there is nothing you need. You may freely choose what you choose, and you are not choosing from need, but from freedom. This is also the absence of fear."

That is nice, he thought. And as he sat there, he realized that at that moment he wasn't afraid and didn't need anything.

flying leap

* * *

He sat up in the grass and took off his shoes and socks. He got lost in how the grass felt on his feet and remembered how often in his life he had been so sure that whatever he thought to be true or accurate had been a fact. Not just for him, but in general. That which had been in his mind he had believed to be applicable to the rest of the world, or at least that part of the world that was as intelligent and normal as him. It had been a very isolated existence that had not allowed for a lot of room. And in a way it had made him a navel gazer. Yet now he felt there was a strange blending of his inside world and the world out there going on. "I am wondering that if there is no world out there *really*, then how can there be an 'in here?' " he wondered out loud.

"Well, once you move further into the experience that you have been having, the boundaries in the old way become more fluid," the bird said. "You find your Self to be no longer limited, as something that is separate from your self here if you will—"

"Hang on!" he interrupted. "What do you mean when you differentiate between the 'Self' and the 'self' like that? I thought my ego was dying and on the way out—and if the ego's gone, isn't that larger Self all that is left, which is to say the field, because it is part and parcel with it? But where does the ego go then? Isn't it part of the field as well? You have said repeatedly that we and every thing is part of the field, so what about the ego?"

The bird was just looking at him without any discernable reaction. Then it shuffled. "You are attempting to conceptualize that which cannot be conceptualized. There are so many things in the way of that: words for one, then the considerable limitation of your thinking, your human form and consciousness ... "

His head was swimming a little now.

"Let it swim, but also know and recognize that this swimming is a direct result of you trying to make that which you are seeing fit into the logic of your ego, where it doesn't belong—the ego you will always have, as a matter of fact, at least as long as you intend to have this human experience."

"So the goal of all this is not to get rid of the ego? What about all that talk about my ego dying and being at my funeral?"

"If you had *listened*, you would not find yourself confused." The bird sneezed one of its sizeable sneezes and sat down in the grass.

"Gesundheit."

"Thank you. So let me remind you of a few things that might help. You do recall that I told you about the usefulness of the ego? How it helps you be human, to have this individuated self experience?"

He nodded.

"It lets you be in the body, use your brain, remember how to do things, how to know language, walk, run, sit, do your job, drive a car … this is the natural and practical function of an ego. It can retain information and maintain the individuated form that you are whilst being human. Without it you could not have this existence as a human. The most important part in all this is the realization that you get to live *with* your ego rather than *as* your ego." The bird fluffed its feathers. "Big difference," it added.

"But what about all those gurus and sages whose books I've read that claim they have moved beyond ego? Are they all full-of-shit liars?"

"Take away the judgment, and you make an accurate observation. To claim not to have any ego is in antithesis to having one. It is a statement of duality and a statement about where that person is in their awareness, still living and measuring within the realm of the duality. To say that you have no ego is the most egotistical thing you could possibly say."

But how did this make sense? If he had indeed become aware of his massive ego, was letting it die, but at the same time kept it around for practical reason as it were, then where was the enlightenment? How could any human being ever become enlightened?

"They can't."

"What? Are you kidding me? What about Buddha, what about Jesus Christ for that matter? They sound pretty enlightened to me! Now I think you're full of it … "

"Slow down! I simply answered your question as to whether a *human being* could be enlightened."

"Yeah, so?"

"Well, Buddha and Jesus were fully *awakened* while in their human form and when they actually moved into their full enlightenment, they left their human form and became light. Within human form, you cannot be fully enlightened. It is an impossibility. You can however live an enlightened *life*, by virtue of becoming fully aware of your Self, the field within and without which all exists, and having full awareness of the natural role your ego plays in your ability to have the human experience. It's really very simple."

"Back up the truck here—so what we can do as human beings is limited in scope so to speak?"

The bird nodded.

"So what we're saying here is that we can become fully aware of how things work, aware of the field, our Self and self, the balance of all that, and by doing so our lives become enlightened, but we as a human being are not, because when we do we evaporate into light?"

The bird chuckled. "That is a great way to put that, 'evaporate.' Actually comes pretty close."

"But then what is the *point* of it all? And I mean the *all*, at least as far as I understand it right now." He waved his arms around in a big circle.

The bird watched him. "Which by virtue of your current state is not much. However, within this very limited context in which we have met and are having this conversation, I can say that the point to it all is creation, period. It is creation expressed through choice. Without creation and choice, nothing would exist, and without anything existing, there is only nothing, which then remains unexperienced."

Man, this was so far off his chart. The ego was not the issue in and of itself, it was the unconsciousness and unawareness of it that was the issue. He did like the way the bird had put it, describing the difference between living *with* your ego as opposed to *as* your ego. That much made sense to him. All it took was a little change in preposition. With this contemplation, the peace returned immediately, his mind calmed down, and the present moment came back into view, into his experience. And this experience was enough. More than enough. He could see himself sitting in the grass and simply being for hours. Everything was illuminated. Not by light per se, but somehow brighter, more vibrant. It was more alive. Like it had a light within.

"Every thing is en-light-ened," the bird said.

* * *

It was indeed; he just had never thought of that word this way before, had never experienced the world like this before. It still felt somewhat strange, the way a new suit felt right after he put it on the first time. On the one hand, he felt really great in it, but the feel of the new fabric, the way the jacket felt around his shoulders and how the pants were riding on him, was still new. He had to laugh at that. It did fit the sensation though.

This awareness of everything really was cool; he hoped it would stick around. This is what he had strived for ultimately, underneath his massive ego story and all its abusive and calculating ways that had been his desire. He could now see how that desire had been channeled by his identification with his ego, always funneled and directed in ways that kept him away from the one thing that would have shown him what he was looking for: the present moment. How ironic. He wondered what he had done differently to finally wake up.

"You were ready to die," the bird said.

That was true. He had been no longer willing to

151

continue his life the way he had lived up until he had
stood on that rooftop. Only he didn't have to physically die—he had run into this bird and had been
presented with another option. It felt as though it
had been a lifetime ago. Time. What was the deal
with that from his new perspective?

"How does time fit in all this?" he wondered out
loud.

"You're kidding, right?" the bird burst out.

"No, I'm not. It's just, well, you know, I've been
feeling all this 'field' stuff and being present and all
that, and I just don't know how time *does* fit in."

The bird stared at him in silence.

"What?"

"Well, why don't you give it a try, all on your
own." The bird picked at his ear and then proceeded
to parade around him.

So he lay there in the grass and looked into the
beautiful blue sky with its puffy popcorn clouds and
let his soul dangle. Time ... how did it fit? Well, first
off, if there were a field—and by now he was pretty
sure that's what he was feeling—and this field contained the "all of everything" all at the same time, in
this eternal Now ...

At that moment he realized he had "known" all
that shit before, that he had even talked about it before, but that he had never really felt it like this.

With the feeling it was different to think about, more real. Like once you learn to swim, the thought of swimming becomes very different from the theoretical concept of swimming you had before entering the water.

With that in his mind he felt as though time was the same as the field. It was something you swam in in every direction—it only *seemed* to move in a straight arrow, and that worked well for, say, doing your laundry. But at the same time it was every time, temporally speaking. He had never thought of it that way, and as he did, his mind felt tickled again just the way it had when he had looked at the night sky so many years before, except it was as though that had just happened.

"That is a very interesting way to describe the idea of time."

"Let's walk," he said.

He found himself profoundly satisfied. He knew he wasn't making much sense, but that was fine; it was really nice not to have the constant babble of important nothings about himself on his mind. It was then that he became conscious of what a drain he had been, how much energy he had wasted.

"Time is much as you described it a moment ago: accessible in all directions, all the time. Let us simply look at this world in a different way when it comes to

153

time. Have you ever thought about all the processes that are going on at any given moment?"

"How do you mean?"

"Well, just think about the number of cells in your body that are splitting themselves up at any moment, the number of particles traveling through and within your body at any moment ... think about the number of trees, all the flowers, the people, every single thought that every single human being is having at any moment, every sand pebble on every beach; the air moving around, all the drops in the ocean moving, every particle and wave of matter moving about at any moment. There are billions of them—"

"Trillions."

"Yes, and—"

"Gazillions!"

"Yes, so—"

"Gazillions upon gazillions!"

The bird stared him down. "Sorry, I was just really getting excited about trying to fathom this ... "

"Obviously. May I continue now?"

"Yes, please," he said.

"The point is that they are countless—that it is literally impossible to count them. How could you fit something that is countless, that cannot have a number to it, into a moment, a time span, no matter how short or long you try to make it?"

Well, that was impossible; there was no way to measure this in time. There wasn't enough or too little time to measure it in. Literally. "Well, in that sense, you could also never measure all the time that has existed since it began; how would you know where or when to start counting, and what would that even mean?" he pondered. "I mean, what if time didn't have a beginning? I can't conceptualize that. What if it did have a beginning? What was there before time existed? I can't conceptualize that, either."

"Which is precisely my point. Time as you think of it in human terms does not actually exist beyond those terms. It is only observable in your time/space continuum and even within that it falls apart conceptually when you begin to look at it in detail. Just think about how a fly that lives only one day experiences time. How about a turtle that turns two hundred years old? Time, in other words, is fluid. You are literally swimming in it. And it is not until you gain perspective—and through that, awareness—that this deeper reality becomes experiential to you. Time as you explain it to one another is simply a function of your state of awareness. Once awareness shifts, time shifts as well."

Another one of those humdingers that he couldn't quite comprehend but that made sense anyway. With that he was thrust back into the moment and realized that they had walked quite a ways and that he was really hungry. Where had the time gone?

"Exactly," the bird said.

* * *

He looked around and tried to get his bearings; he wasn't sure where he was, they hadn't gone *that* far, but yet everything was unfamiliar. He stopped on the street corner and really began to check things out. It felt as though his brain was having a hard time processing all the information around him, or at least the information that made it possible to figure out where he was. It was a very strange sensation, but then again, strange was becoming normal. He finally recognized a building across the street and from that realized that he was actually not far from his office, and that he had spent a lot of time in this area in the past few years. Yet he didn't recognize most of the buildings; he would have sworn that they had been dropped here in the past week. How absolutely, positively strange and oddly invigorating this felt. So he stood there and began to look at all those 'new' buildings and really enjoyed it.

His focus then shifted to all the people around him. Every single one of them had a palpable energy. They were rushing around, on their way to somewhere, talking on their phones, texting, eating—all the usual stuff people did when they were out and about. He saw all this but could also feel their busyness. How funny that "business" was so close to "busyness" in more ways than just the spelling. A guy dressed with lots of bling and an attitude to match stood waiting to cross the street. But what he saw for some reason was this really nice and funny guy.

The guy noticed him. "What the fuck you lookin' at?"

He hadn't expected that, and the first thing out of his mouth was: "Well, you."

The guy looked at him, not quite sure. "I *see* that motherfucker. Do you have a problem?"

He wasn't scared, just curious. "Not really, no, you just look very interesting."

He couldn't believe he'd just said that.

"What the fuck you talkin' 'bout, man? How about I pump some lead in your ass and make sure your eyesight gets corrected?" With that the guy lifted his shirt and flashed a gun.

And then the strangest thing happened: he saw this man across from him, but rather than seeing the menace, the threat, he saw this young guy and his ego in all its glory, and how it was running his show, and how scared shitless his ego was all the time. It was clear as day. He had no judgment about him whatsoever—he simply *saw* him in his totality.

And underneath all that ego, he saw the same feeling he had been experiencing all day.

"Well, you could do that, of course," he said. "You are clearly equipped for the task. But may I suggest that my eyesight is just fine, and that you would be wasting your bullets, and also that you would scare the shit out of my bird … " He tilted his head towards the bird who was resting on his shoulder.

The guy looked at him and then laughed. "Whatever you're on brother, I want some of that." He dropped his shirt and looked at the bird. "What's up with the air rat anyway? Don't they spread disease and shit?" And with that he walked away laughing.

Well, that had been interesting.

"Your new perspective comes with that. You can experience everything beyond and before the label. That is exactly how you saw him. You saw beyond the physical form, beyond the ego form. It is like a sort of X-ray vision that gives you the ability to see right through the layers of the obvious form and tune into the frequency of that which is underneath."

"The field," he said quietly. He knew exactly what the bird was talking about. He had seen the guy in layers very clearly, and once he had looked beyond that ego, he recognized the field, kind of within him but not exactly either; it was shining through, but it also had *been* the guy at the same time. And with

158

seeing that came the same feeling he had been experiencing with himself, in the park. So this shit was really everywhere, wasn't it? Literally *everywhere* at all times.

"I knew this as a kid," he said to himself. "I knew that there was this energy to things, that there was nothing that could limit this energy and therefore nothing could limit me." He remembered back to the days when he would play make-believe and inhabit whole worlds in his mind. "It was normal then you know." He glanced at the bird with a reminiscent smile. "It was as though the adults were the crazy and bitter ones, they were the ones with the problems, the frowned faces, the fights, not us—not me. It wasn't until I was probably five or six that that part of my life began to shrink, and with it the feeling ... "

"That's when the story became you. Your ego began to take up residence in your being and, in your case, grew into the monster you have witnessed. And you are quite correct about the child's mind. It is very much aware of its place, aware of the field that it is as well, and within that space, anything is possible." The bird flew up and landed on his other shoulder, messing up his hair. "Most adults will teach their kids these beautiful things: they tell them not to lie, to be kind to others, to share, and—most importantly—they tell them to dream. They encourage this, because they remember how beautiful it was for them when they could dream. And those same parents go out into the 'real world' to do whatever it is that they do, and they lie, and they're not very kind, they don't share freely, and most of all, they don't dream."

This was so clear to see now. "And we justify it by telling ourselves that this is how things are in the 'real world,' that kids can count themselves lucky to be kids for as long as they can. And yet we never wonder about what we teach them and how we behave in the very next second because everyone is addicted to their egos and stories." He looked at the people around him again and could see the weight of their stories in their faces and bodies. Two days ago he had been in similar shoes. What a difference a couple of days could make, a couple of moments.

"There is no reason why anything on this planet should ever die but for natural causes and what you might call an 'accident,'" the bird said. "The very ego we have been talking about, the one you have been living your life as, this ego is the reason for all remaining deaths. The ego causes the disconnect between people that enables them to commit the atrocities they do. It is ego that drives the need and greed for things and thus the impetus to steal and take. It creates the jealousy that makes people want to control another. It is the reason why people envy, hate, and love in that way that says 'This is mine.' It is the reason why people can feel so lonely that they want to kill another person to silence the pain or even kill themselves."

He saw clearly in his mind's eye what the bird was describing in its totality. Being the ego was the root of all the discord on the planet, no matter its form. Living *with* one's ego changed it all. It was so simple. And powerful.

His story was disappearing, his concern for the future was dissolving, his past may as well have been someone else's. But without any of those elements, what was he now?

"Being." The bird nudged him in the ear.

* * *

"But this seems so easy, so natural. I mean, I am still here and all that, but I just feel different, lighter maybe, and everything around me is just there. But in its 'thereness' it's so cool to look at—no, it's so cool to experience. It's like having that natural high when you are on vacation for the first day in a new place and everything is so fresh and interesting. That's almost what this feels like, only better. But is that 'being'?"

"Of course it is. As I have said before, it's not re-

ally a big deal once you are in the actuality of being, but it is the most 'real' you will ever feel and be.
Everything is indeed new to you again and again,
because you step outside of time by virtue of not at-
taching yourself to a story. Once the story goes, the
memory goes. And I am talking about the memory
of creating a separate identity of 'you' here, not the
practical memories of functioning in your body and
within this time/space continuum. That's not who
you are, that is what you *use* to have your human
experience."

Well, if that was all true—and it felt like it was—
then where did memories of a lifetime fit in? He was
still able to remember things from his life. But it
didn't have a feeling attached to it like it used to.

"That's exactly my point. Once you no longer *are*
your memories, they are simply memories. You may
recall them, but you don't have to hold on to them
as tightly as you can, so you won't lose your identity
and self."

Now that was throwing a whole different light on
the concept of "making memories," wasn't it? Even in
his old life it had struck him odd to what extent people obsessed with taking pictures or recording vid-
eos; some were looking at their lives almost entirely
through the screen on the back of their camera—all
in the name of "capturing the moment," of "making

memories." And in the process they were not actually experiencing the moment. They were literally trying to make the very memories that would create a sense of self, of story, as if to say "I have existed," trying to create permanence in an impermanent world. It was like trying to save the Titanic by spooning out the water. And life just passed by that way. And then everyone would sit and look at those memories in whatever form and remember a life that was not us to begin with. Now that was hard.

"Yes, it sure doesn't sound like a joyful life to me," the bird chimed in. "This is, however, how most humans live, and it creates the very world you've just observed; a world full of memory making and clinging to them for dear life, for without those memories, 'who are we?' people ask. And they call those memories religion, culture, ethnicity, nation, history, tradition, 'the good old days,' and on and on it goes. And in the name of protecting those memories, people hurt each other in countless ways, from a hurtful remark to all-out war. For if you take away memories, you take away me."

He thought of the countless arguments over how something had happened, whether it had been or not been, arguments about arguments and how they had or had not happened. But it really didn't matter at all, did it? The only reality was *now*, nothing else.

163

flying leap

And even in this now, everyone was having their own experience of it, the one they were creating at that particular moment, in their own individual way; how could memories ever be accurate if in that sense the present wasn't even accurate? Even memories changed all the time. Hell, depending on his mood, the same memory could be completely different.

"It makes me wonder though what I am if my memories aren't me, but simply memories. Where does that leave *me*? What are we, if not our memories?" And before the bird could even react: "I did pay attention and know that I am that Self, that I am aware and more consciously part of that field ... but I am a little lost as to what the point of my existence may be. Without my memories, I am just here."

"Of course you are here. And you also *are*. You are an individuated form that experiences the field, in order for it to experience itself. The point of any existence of any thing is simply said: creation expressed through choice. You choose yourself, you choose yourself in countless ways in every moment of what you call your life. There is nothing you can do about that fact. It is the way the Universe is designed. As a human experience you have the ability to be what you are being right now: conscious. The field pervades every thing. There is no thing and no where the field is not. So every thing is the field, but not every thing may be or can be *conscious* of this, except for humans—at least around here."

They walked further down the block. "What do you mean by that?"

"Well, as I have mentioned a few times before, the field or creation expresses itself in *limitless and infinite* ways, so with that in mind, did you think that this planet—or for that matter, this time/space continuum—was the only place in existence?"

Damn, the bird *had* said that before. How could he ever understand this, how much *was* infinite or limitless, really?

"Think a hundred thousand billion gazillion multiplied by ten trillion with a factor of a hundred gazillion, and you're not even close," the bird said with what he could swear was a shit grin on its face.

* * *

He sat down on a retaining wall and caught his mind. On the one hand, everything was making sense to him; on the other hand, nothing did. In all of this, he felt calm and alive. Not even particularly good or happy, just so alive. This was what he had always wanted to feel, what he had waited for his entire life. He also knew that he had thought that same thought since meeting the bird, but it was changing every time and getting more *real* every time and he knew that this was only going to continue from now on.

"Probably so, my friend, but I guarantee that it will only get better every moment of your life."

"To infinity," he chuckled.

"To infinity, because that is all there is." The bird hopped off his shoulder and landed next to him on the wall.

He looked down at it and realized how fond he had grown of this little creature who he knew not to be so little after all. They shared a silent moment.

"Do you realize that because of the design of your human form, having consciousness in the way you do, you are also the only creature that can choose to live finitely?"

"I guess I didn't."

"A plant does not have the same consciousness as humans do, it cannot tell time, it does not live in time actually, it only knows to *exist*, and in that it only knows to be with each eternal moment, regardless of any circumstance. It does not learn how to grow, it simply grows; it does not die, it does not want, it does not experience loss when the plant next to it dies, because there is no death. No animal feels sadness about dying or remorse about killing, they do not experience loss, they do not experience fear—though some of your scientists have postulated that they do. What they have observed, they have always interpreted from a human standpoint. They give human labels to natural reactions. In reality, animals do not feel the *human* sense of loss, sadness, right or wrong, happy or sad—anything that is a duality. And do you know why?"

"Because they do not have an awareness of themselves as separate from anything. We start out the same way, don't we?"

"Yes, you could say that, but your design is different, because you develop a sense of separateness so that you may experience your Self, which is the field. An animal or plant is not designed that way; they never leave infinity, they are infinity. Because they do not live *in* time, they simply live *with* it. Every thing on your planet lives infinitely, except you, though you do feel it at times, and are reminded of it. You get to choose whether you want to live in full, partial, or no awareness of this. When you move beyond your story, you move into infinity quite naturally."

"And if I live in this experience of infinity, I never die. Because there is no beginning or end—"

"Because there is no death. It does not exist in infinity."

"So in reality I don't ever die. I simply move from this state of my experience as a human, with all the laws of this world and its physics, into a different state. And since I am part of the field, actually am the field, I am part of the whole deal all the time, whether I recognize it or not, whether I believe it or not. I can make up anything I want about anything then."

"Absolutely."

"So I am made up as well?"

"Continuously. As long as you choose to."

"What about you?"

"What about me?"

"When we met, I asked you whether you were God, and you said something like 'in a way I am, but not the way you think of that right now.' "

"Close enough."

"Well?"

"Well, what?" And he knew that the bird was waiting for him, waiting for him to see something, to say something, to do something that would bring it all together. "So you are God *and* you're not is what I'm getting here. In all the time that we have been together I have learned and am beginning to feel that there is this field—hell, I am beginning to see it. And we have also talked about the field as only one way to describe that which cannot be described. You mentioned that there are many different ways to talk about this field, that we could call it God or Bud-

168

dha, or Allah, or the Supreme Intelligence, the Big Bang, the Great Nothing—anything and everything that we as human beings have ever come up with to describe this, the one thing we cannot describe but know is there … " He was almost out of breath.

The bird just sat there. There was more and he knew it. He looked at the clouds and let his mind relax. "It's all made up though, all of it, everything I just described has simply been made up, and then we turn it into a story, a collective story at that, and after a while no one questions it anymore, no one ever stops to listen to themselves, to their Self, so we live in these stories in complete ignorance and we create our worlds based on this information … on information that we made up in the first place and continue to make up over and over again, only to distract ourselves from the very reality that we are in fact infinite and that there is *nothing to fear*."

"Very nice my friend." He felt the bird and could see that it was as much the field as everything else. And then he understood.

"You and I are made up, as everything is. If I am of the field, so are you; I am you and you are me." He started to cry at that moment, because it hit him like all the bricks of the house of the Universe were raining down on him.

"I have been talking to me all this time. And everyone else is, too; it just depends on whether we are listening."

With that, the bird just looked at him, nodded and flew away.

"Right you are," he heard himself and the bird say together in his mind. "It is all One."

* * *

After sitting on the wall for a while he realized what he had to do. He went home, got out his laptop, and started to type:

Jump

"He glanced down; it seemed a lot higher up than from below. Funny, how things changed with a simple shift of perspective. Perspective. That was something to consider … "